They've loved each other since childhood. Marriage has always been their destiny. But lately they've lost a fragile balance between them. Now he's given himself a deadline to win her back or lose her forever.

Sam and Megan have been soulmates, best friends, and sweethearts since they were kids living next door to each other. Twenty years. "Two peas in a pod." Everyone in Cordial Creek, Vermont, expects thirty-year-old Sam, an architect, and twenty-eight-year-old Megan, a paralegal, to tie the knot. They were about to do that until the untimely death of Sam's dad, two years ago, devastated Sam and settled him even deeper into the small town he loves. He threw himself into his construction company and took on new responsibilities as his mother's shoulder-to-lean-on. Megan adores him but is struggling with the changes in their relationship—and with some doubts about herself that she can't quite identify.

One small, reckless mistake on her part—a silly ploy to shake Sam out of his doldrums—explodes into a painful turning point. He sets out to remind her of all the special bonds they share, and why they're perfect together. If the memories don't solve Megan's crisis, all the little things that they love about each other may not be enough to keep them together.

Other Novels by Heidi Sprouse

Coming Soon

Lightning Can Strike Twice

Adirondack Sundown

All the Little Things

by

Heidi Sprouse

Bell Bridge Books

⹂B

Bell Bridge Books
PO BOX 300921
Memphis, TN 38130
Print ISBN: 978-1-61194-402-0

Bell Bridge Books is an Imprint of BelleBooks, Inc.

Copyright © 2013 by Heidi Sprouse

Printed and bound in the United States of America.

We at BelleBooks enjoy hearing from readers.
Visit our websites – www.BelleBooks.com and www.BellBridgeBooks.com.

10 9 8 7 6 5 4 3 2 1

Cover design: Debra Dixon
Interior design: Hank Smith
Photo/Art credits:
Scene (manipulated) © Gergely Zsolnai | Dreamstime.com

:Ltlp:01:

Dedication

To my husband, Jimmy, who knows everything about me, big and small, and loves me anyway!

To my son, Patrick, who started out as something little but is the greatest gift I will ever have.

To anyone looking for love:

You might think that the moment you fall in love will be an earthquake, a tidal rush, in a spectacular place, or you'll be doing something out of this world. Maybe you've imagined that it will be something about that person that just hits you over the head, shouting, "This is the one!"

*Real life, real **love**, doesn't happen that way. It isn't BIG or over the top . . . it will be the things most wouldn't notice, the inconsequential details, the events others would overlook. It will be all of the little things that you'll never forget because they only happened with her, they only belong to her—and you as well. All of those little things will add up to prove that she is your everything. My advice to you—pay close attention, or you might miss it.*

Someone you can trust,
Sam O'Malley

1

Just Out for a Sunday Drive

IN RETROSPECT, Sam kept noticing all the little things about that fateful day. It was a Sunday. A beautiful, sunny, not-a-cloud- in-the-sky kind of Sunday in Cordial Creek, Vermont. The kind of day that made a person want to stop time, freeze it, stick it in a pocket to keep it forever. So bright that it stabbed at his eyes, made him squint and grab for his sunglasses. He always forgot his sunglasses.

Even though it was autumn, the sun took the chill off, settled like a blanket on the air, made coats fall off and short sleeves come out of the closet. It also begged for classic cars to come out of the garage. Sam put the top down on his vintage, cherry red, 1963 Corvette roadster. More little things—the long list of details about a car—but vital to a car enthusiast. It felt good to drive out and meet the day with nothing between him and the wind tugging at his hair and clothes, filling him with a sense of freedom.

MEGAN TAYLOR woke up early that morning, before the sun. Stared up at the ceiling with dry eyes. Watched the dawn creep in, splashing the walls in a wash of pink, red, gold. She climbed out of bed and made a pot of tea. Like she did, every single morning, work day or not.

Scalded her tongue but drank it down with fingers that trembled. It was Sunday. People were supposed to look forward to Sunday, so what was the matter with her?

The newspaper remained on the kitchen table, unopened except for the comics, in search of something, anything light-hearted. Her shower stretched until the water ran cold. In a soft, terrycloth robe in hurt-your-eyes red, she stood by the mirror and dried her hair until it was a golden mass of curls gleaming down her back. Sam loved her hair, would run his fingers through it, press his face to it when they held each other close. Thoughts of Sam made her want to cry. It was no fault of his own; the problem rested in Meg.

She changed her clothes twice, three times, stood in front of the floor length, antique mirror that had been her grandmother's. Stepped into heels that hurt her feet but made her legs look good; some insensitive man had probably invented the torture devices. Turned once, took one more slow turn, glanced over her shoulder. Blue eyes—*cerulean; that was the color on the crayon box*—stared back at her, shocking in their intensity. Questioning. It all hung in the balance, what she was doing today. It was a gamble, a chance she was willing to take. Still made her feel shaky, made her doubt her sanity.

Megan stood in the kitchen and watched the clock. Her heart hammered in time with its ticking. Today would be a first for her, something she'd read about, seen in the movies, but never had to do. Her stomach was flip-flopping. She closed her eyes and breathed in and out through her nose, striving to settle everything down when the purr of an engine made her eyes snap open again. She'd know that sound anywhere; Sam, come to pick her up, in the Corvette. She hadn't warned him, couldn't talk to him, didn't know what she would say. Time to find out. She swallowed hard, afraid.

ONLY ONE thing could make this day perfect—spending it with his girl. Sam didn't have to tell her he was coming; this was their Sunday routine. The sweet hum of the Corvette's engine announced his arrival. Megan came to the door in a cute little dress that was a splash of fall colors, hues of orange, red, and yellow setting a fire in his veins. He wondered later, should the dress, on a lazy, Sunday afternoon when she usually wore jeans, have tipped him off? Or the forced smile as she slid in next to him and barely brushed his cheek with her lips? He started a conversation, had a few brief responses, and let the silence take over. Maybe she wanted to be quiet, enjoy the day, like he did. He only wanted to take in the sights . . . and her.

The road stretched out before them, filled with twists and turns—more foreshadowing of what was to come? When it came to their relationship, Sam saw one lane running straight into a blazing sunrise of a future. A little girl with sunshine in her hair and the sky in her eyes, like Megan. A tyke of a boy, a miniature Sam, with dark waves of unruly brown hair and coffee eyes, toddling to keep up. A cozy house that would reach out and tuck them in with two rockers on the porch to grow gray in . . .

They pulled up to a four-way stop at an intersection when Sam's vision hit a dead end. In a blink, Megan was out of the car, walking away as fast as her high heels—*she only wears heels to work or special occasions* flashed through his mind—could carry her. Frozen until the beat of his heart started again, Sam jumped out, left the car door open and the motor running. Horns blared. People yelled and made rude gestures. Others stopped to watch the soap opera. Sam caught up with her, long legs easily closing the gap, and grabbed her arm. "Meg, what is this?"

She turned, tears in her eyes. "I can't do this anymore—one more Sunday drive and I'll go crazy. Sam, I care about you, but let me go. I don't even know how to explain it. I'll tell you later. Call me in the morning." His arm dropped as his fingers turned numb; it felt like something had bitten him, sent a slow poison running through his veins. He remained in the middle of the road, while she continued walking away. Unbelievably, she stepped into a waiting cab. The only cab in Cordial Creek. She'd planned this. It pulled away before Sam could make himself move.

Traffic continued to flow around him, the wind of its passing pushing at him. "Hey, Sam! Out of the road!" a man called.

Red and blue lights flashed—they should mean something. A young officer, solid, with a crew cut and strong jaw, reminded Sam of a marine as he stepped beside him and touched his arm. "Sam, you need to get out of the road. Do you need assistance?"

Switch gears. Focus. Ignore the pounding in his head and stabbing in his chest. Was this having a heart attack? "Yes . . . I mean, no, I don't need help. I lost something . . . out of my car. I'll move my car."

The officer directed traffic, keeping the shell-shocked man in his line of sight at all times. Sam moved as if underwater, in slow motion, and pulled his car to the side of the road. Once there, he didn't move. He didn't have any reason or inclination to go anywhere. He tipped his head back and stared, unseeing, at the clear blue sky trying to figure out what happened.

MEGAN SAT BY the window of the cab, face turned to the glass as the tears flowed. She didn't look back at Sam, couldn't look back at him. Now or never! Her heart was racing until it hurt. Her hands shook in her lap until she clasped them tightly together over her purse. Her eyes were squeezed shut but Sam's face, the shock and the hurt when she got out of the car, told him no more, could not be erased.

She hadn't meant for it to happen that way; her mind had raced for days—no, weeks—in an effort to find a way to tell Sam that she was unhappy and couldn't figure out why. All of her life, she had done the right thing, the predictable, followed the regimented life of a military household. Her relationship with Sam, it had always been there, something that she fell into like falling into bed at night; it was that easy, moving from friendship to something more. Right now, she wanted something spontaneous, the unknown. Sam was the only boyfriend she'd ever had, an old pair of shoes, the only pair she'd worn, comfortable and familiar. She was the only girlfriend he'd ever had. They were on an absolute path to marriage; had been, for years.

What if she made a disappointing wife? An inadequate mother? She had to find out what was tearing her apart inside.

The cab pulled into a small town next door to Cordial Creek. Megan stepped out at a small café, paid the driver, and set up a time for him to return. She wiped her eyes and set her shoulders. Standing by the door was a tall man in a dark suit, eyes hidden by sunglasses, black hair slicked back. Mr. Classic, tall, dark, and handsome. He raised a hand to her in recognition. She returned the gesture. She'd only seen him in a photograph on the online dating site, but she knew it was him.

The road was clear. Butterflies fluttered in her

stomach as she walked across, greeted him, and let him open the café door.

This is a mistake, a huge mistake. I hate his slick hair already. Her heart sank. *Oh, Sam.*

"Are you ready for anything?" His touch sent a chill up her arm, and she wanted to jerk away. New territory here; she wasn't sure how to handle it. She smiled coolly. They set out for a simple get-to-know-you lunch that seemed as sad, mysterious, and terrifying as a trip to another country.

Oh, Sam. What have I done?

2

The Morning . . . Aftermath

IN THE EARLY morning hours, Sam's life was divided into two photographs, sliced down the middle by a stop sign and the slam of a car door. Everything before Megan got out of the Corvette was alive and rich in brilliant color; everything after faded into black and white.

He sat in a chair, in the dark, eyes wide open. He hadn't slept that night, couldn't sleep. There was a painful knot in his stomach, twisting with a vengeance, bringing a bad taste to his mouth. That and a headache at the base of his skull made him feel like his head was about to explode. His blood pressure was probably through the roof, threatening a self-induced stroke. He should go to the hospital, get some drugs, or find oblivion in a bottle.

His mind wouldn't let it go, kept the images rolling from the moment Megan sat down beside him on the white leather seat of his classic car to the instant her feet touched the ground, carrying her away. He couldn't turn off the replay in his head. Time was a punishment, dragging by at a painfully slow pace, and the night wore on. Memory was most cruel, a video stuck in the same spot—yesterday afternoon. Made him watch it over and over, looking for answers.

It didn't make sense to him. Megan had been in his

life for twenty years; they'd met as children, grown up as best friends; becoming a couple had been as easy as breathing. Sam had thought the next step would be marriage. He'd often brought it up, but somehow Megan had avoided the topic. That should have been a red flag.

Instead, they would spend their spare time together at each other's homes; Megan would come by in the morning with wake-up coffee then stop by after work, or Sam would surprise her at her place. The weekends were always something to look forward to, a time for day trips, to get away, to be together.

Was that the problem? Not forcing the issue of a commitment? Too much familiarity? Falling into a routine with no edge to it like two old people, nothing to make her feel alive? Had he made it too comfortable so that it was easier for her to walk away? His thoughts went in circles, sharks snapping vicious jaws. Dawn finally arrived, but he was at a loss as to what to do with the daylight. This really shouldn't be so hard or dramatic. It happened all the time. Boy meets girl. Girl breaks boy's heart. End of story. Tell that to his heart.

The ticking of the clock kept beating on his brain, reminding him that there was something that he had to do. He picked up the phone, dialed, and reached his secretary. Had to clear his throat at the sound of her voice, silently cursing its cracking. *Heaven help me, don't let me lose it.* "Janet, it's Sam. I'm feeling lousy today. When Michael comes in, tell him he's in charge. I'll try to be in tomorrow." None of it was a lie—his voice proved just how lousy he felt. His secretary assured him she'd take care of everything and hoped he'd feel better.

His chair was his refuge, where he remained the rest of the day and into the night, moving only when the demands of the bathroom and thirst required it. No sleep. No food. No relief. He was waiting—for the phone to ring, the door to open, or for merciful sleep to come and erase the last twenty four hours. Being real life, none of those things happened. His eyes burned with the need to rest. His stomach protested with the need to eat. His heart ached with the need to beat again.

Cursing himself, unable to sit still any longer, Sam showered, pulled on jeans and a t-shirt, and peeled out of the driveway in his pickup truck. He went way too fast, kicking up dust on the dirt road, blind to the scenery around him. Destination—anywhere but here, as long as it was out of his mind.

MICHAEL FLANNIGAN pulled in early to the construction site of his latest project, an office building that resembled an old brownstone. He usually was the second one in after his workaholic boss, although he tried to beat him as a personal, daily challenge. He thought he'd finally managed the day before only to find out Sam wasn't coming in. Odd—Sam didn't miss work. Many a time, he'd come in dead on his feet, sicker than a dog. However, today the boss's faded blue, beater Chevy was in its typical spot. Whatever had kept him home couldn't be that serious.

Sighing deeply at having lost the morning race again, Michael sipped his black coffee in an effort to wake up. He tipped his head back and relaxed just for a moment more. Might as well savor the life-restoring properties of good coffee, take a few more minutes. What was the rush? The boss was already there; no chance for brownie points today. Not that he had to anyway. They were partners, and Michael pulled his weight; it was a matter of principle to get there first. Eyes closed to shut out the blaze of sunrise beating directly into his eyes, a loud pounding made its way into his consciousness and had him sitting up with a jolt. He bit his tongue as coffee spilled down the front of his shirt—what a waste!—and jumped out of his truck, a rusted, green monster to rival Sam's in age and condition. His heart picked up the pace, matching the loud thudding that continued. What was going on? Was there trouble at the site? Vandalism had happened before, and no demolition was scheduled for today. Visions of trouble makers, bent on destruction, were supplied by a colorful imagination.

Michael broke out in a cold sweat as he covered his disheveled, black hair with a hard hat. Had to follow the Boy Scout motto, be prepared for anything, by picking up a sledgehammer. He held it down low, close to his side to provide the element of surprise. Just topping off six feet tall, and hard from being outdoors and working construction, he was a force to be reckoned with. That and the fear that Sam might be in trouble resolved Michael to center himself and step out on to the work site, unprepared for what he found.

Sam also hefted a sledgehammer. Not only did he hold it, he was wielding it, making quick work out of destroying one interior wall on their project building. They had been—key word being had—ahead of schedule. Sam's voice was hoarse from yelling, torn with emotion as he shouted with each swing. "Damn it! How could you do this?!" A pause as he wiped dust—and possibly tears?—out of his eyes. "What the hell did I do? What the hell am I supposed to do now?" The force of his rage and anguish sent the hammer flying across the yard. He stood, head bowed, hands on his hips as he tried to slow his breathing. Large and formidable, covered in dust, most would not have approached Sam at that moment. Michael was not most.

"All you had to do was tell us if you weren't happy

with that wall," Michael told his best friend, hoping humor would help salvage the pieces of whatever wreckage buried Sam. He had to look up; Sam topped him by a few inches and wouldn't let Michael forget it.

Sam met his old friend's gaze; a sea of pain crashed in his eyes, taking Michael's breath away. Not the boss of anything at that moment, especially himself, Sam walked away into the shell of the building until he reached the opposite wall. He sank down onto the floor and pressed his head to his knees.

Completely at a loss, Michael did the only thing he could do—he followed. He had been Sam's shadow since they were kids. They'd seen each other through all of the minor scrapes through the years and the big ones, the heart-stopping, bring-the-world-to-a-halt-moments; looked like this might be one of them. Nothing had changed with the years. His friend was in trouble; Michael was there. He sat down beside him and rested an arm on Sam's shoulders.

It was like holding onto a rock, muscles clenched so tightly with tension he was shaking. Michael held on anyway. "Tell me. What happened?" Sam was strong, carried the load when others put it down. Michael didn't like what he saw in his friend's eyes.

Sam shied away from the comfort offered. He looked into deep, green eyes that he knew almost as well as his own and saw only calm waiting for him. Wished he could have one small piece of it. Sam looked away. "I can't right now. I'm sorry, but I just can't."

They didn't talk for several minutes; the sound of Sam's harsh breathing was the only thing between them. Michael cleared his throat. "The guys are going to be here any minute, Sam. Why don't you take off? I've got it covered."

His friend barely nodded. "Thanks," he whispered

then stood up and walked out, head bowed. Michael was right to tell him to go. He wouldn't be good for anyone.

MEGAN CALLED into work Monday morning. A brass band was blasting inside a head that weighed at least one hundred pounds. Too much wine. What had possessed her to drink an entire bottle of wine? Sam's face and the hurt that bloomed in his eyes floated to the surface of her mind, and she covered her head with a pillow, tried to drown it out. She'd seen him every time the stranger at the café offered to fill her glass.

She didn't know what she was looking for, and it was driving her crazy. Tossing and turning in a tangle of sheets, stomach pitching along with her pounding headache, she couldn't escape the fact that all thoughts returned to the man she'd been trying to forget . . . her childhood sweetheart. Was it possible to meet your true love as a child and make it last? As a girl, that had been the fairy tale, but somewhere along the way, Megan stopped believing in pixie dust, Tinker Bell, Peter Pan, or happily ever after.

Flinging back the covers, she ended up on the bathroom floor, clinging to the toilet as her stomach rebelled. Everything made a return appearance, possibly every meal she'd ever eaten in her life. When it was over and she was reduced to a shaking, sniffling mess, Megan stretched out on the cold tile and did what every girl did when she'd made a mess out of her life . . . she cried her eyes out.

3

Rising to the Challenge

SAM DIDN'T remember the ride home or when he started walking or for how long. The skies opened up, pouring down buckets on his bare head. Made him shiver, set his teeth to chattering, and he didn't care. How fitting for his present situation and mood. He made no conscious decision, yet his feet carried him down the mile-long path that wound through the woods between his house and Megan's. She'd been so excited when she was able to buy a place; it had been so convenient, as if it fell into her lap, just a shout away from Sam. Meant to be, that's what she had said. It was torture now, so close but so far away. Right now, it felt like there was a wide ocean, filled with rough waters, gaping between them.

Her door pulled at him like a magnet. His feet carried him up the steps when his mind told him to turn around, go home, get drunk. Anything but this. He had to be stupid, a glutton for punishment. His hand pounded the wood until it shook; if he could've sent his fist through the heavy oak, he would have.

The door was yanked open. "What's the meaning of this . . . oh, Sam." Megan's eyes opened wide as she took in his appearance. He looked like something out of a nightmare, hair plastered to his head, mud on his shoes, a darkness lurking in his eyes that was frightening.

Usually a rich brown like hot chocolate and equally sweet, they were almost black. Lightning illuminated the sky, only intensifying the overall effect.

How could she look . . . normal . . . in jeans and a t-shirt with her hair pulled back, like everything was okay? Like the world wasn't coming to an end around them. "I have one question. Why?" Sam stood his ground and stared her down, waiting for an answer.

Megan glanced down at her bare feet with shiny, pink nail polish sprucing up her toes. She'd had time to paint her nails? "I wrote it in the note," came out in a meek whisper.

His hands came up of their own will and grasped her shoulders. *Breathe in, breathe out. Don't lose it.* "I didn't read it. I want to hear you say it."

Somehow, she knew it would come to this. She usually faced her problems head on—it was a Taylor trait, inbred from the army blood in her veins—but didn't know how to do it with Sam. There was too much between them, the pain would go too deep, and how to begin? And so, she had tried to make the break, clean and quick—they said that was the best way with bones. Why not with hearts?

She'd already written the note before Sam picked her up Sunday afternoon and had planned on delivering it while Sam went to his mother's for dinner; after her lunch date, still flustered and reeling from her outing, Megan had hurried over to Sam's. It had been a relief when he was not home, to take the coward's way out and drop the envelope on his bed. She regretted it now.

"Come in," she told him quietly. His hands fell to his sides, and Megan padded softly into the living room where she curled up in a recliner with her feet tucked beneath her. She tried to make herself as small as she felt at this moment. Running away, being anywhere but here, would be preferable.

Good manners drilled in by Sam's parents would not be ignored. He removed his dirty shoes even though he had the perverse urge to trek mud on her cream-colored carpet, hung up his coat with shaking fingers, and wiped away some of the dirt on his jeans. A mess. She had made a royal mess of him, and it infuriated him that he'd let someone have that power over him. That and the fact that betrayal had come from the one closest to his heart was killing him. He joined Megan in the living room and sat on the end of the sofa that was closest to her. He refused to make this easy on her. Lightning lit the window behind them and thunder boomed loudly enough to make her jump. Perfect. The outside matched Sam's insides. He hoped she would feel as wretched as he did. "Say it."

"I . . . I felt trapped, like I was going nowhere. Here I was, driving down the same, old roads, living in the same town, working the same job, seeing the same faces every day and with the same man . . . nothing new, nothing different. My scenery hasn't changed for twenty years! One day, I looked around and I wondered—is this it? And how do I know that you and I are really meant to be if I've never known anything else? I feel suffocated, and if I go on one more *Sunday drive* I'm going to go out of my mind! I want to climb Mount Everest or fly to Vegas on a weeknight and call in the next day. I want to dance in the rain and go to Europe or on a cruise. I need to go places, do things, see something more than Cordial Creek, Vermont. I need . . . I don't know what, but I need to find out."

Sam closed his eyes, trying to shut it all out. He couldn't understand. What had always been a comfort to him—knowing his place, their shared history—had become a prison to her? She'd never said anything before, never even hinted that they were in trouble. Something pricked at the edge of his mind . . . something from their Sunday drive. "When I picked you up, you were in a dress. What's the reason for the dress?"

So, he had noticed. Of course, he noticed everything about her. "I was meeting someone for lunch," Megan mumbled softly.

"You . . . met a *man?*"

She couldn't look at him either, and her cheeks suddenly burned. "I set it up through an internet dating service."

Sam was out of the chair in an instant, pacing with one hand raking through his hair while he pointed accusingly at her with the other. "You have got to be kidding me! You left me for a stranger picked out by a computer?"

Megan stared down at her hands now clasped around her knees. Listening to him, she heard just how ridiculous it all sounded. "It seemed the easiest way. Besides, short of leaving town, how can I meet anyone? I know everyone here!"

"What's his name? No, I don't want to know. Was that the first time you saw him?"

Megan stood up and started doing some pacing of her own. "Yes. We spoke on the phone a few times before Sunday. That was it."

"Let me get this straight. You decided to throw away everything we have based on a few conversations with a stranger, and never thought to talk to me first?" He turned away. His fist slammed against a wooden post. The bloom of pain was a welcome distraction, a fraction of how she'd hurt him. He pressed his head to the solid pine, despair weighing him down. What had he hoped to accomplish by coming here?

It made her heart ache, watching him. Megan

stopped pacing and tentatively laid a hand on Sam's back. His muscles instantly became a taut rope beneath her touch. "I didn't know how to tell you that something was wrong with us . . . or with me, anyway. I couldn't see someone else while I was with you. I could never do that to you."

Sam shook his head, his voice broken. "You're just so damned considerate, Meg."

She stepped closer and wrapped her arms around his waist. "I'm sorry, Sammy. I don't want to hurt you. I just don't know what else to do. I need a break, to figure out what I want."

Sam whipped around and took her hands in his. "Listen to me. Take your break. But give me . . . twenty days, one day for each year that you've been in my life. Let me prove that what you want was here all along. If it doesn't work, I'll let you go. I'll hate it, but I'll do it."

Megan was filled with doubt. "Sam, can't we just sit down and talk about everything? I don't know, Sam. I can't think straight . . ."

He dipped down and kissed her, a fierce kiss, possessive and laying claim. It was filled with hurt, passion, and anger. "Twenty days, Meg. You owe me that." He didn't wait for an answer. He turned, grabbed his coat, and stepped into his boots before meeting the night. The rain continued to pour down without reprieve as he made the journey home.

Megan remained where he left her, rooted to the spot by the power of his kiss. The kiss and the man that left her had been strangers to her. That was not the boy of her childhood nor the man that had become as comfortable as her favorite pair of jeans. What had she unleashed? She wondered if this was how Pandora felt when she opened the box.

She went to bed early that night. After two days of

calling in, she couldn't push it for a third; people would be showing up, bringing chicken soup and sympathy that wasn't deserved. Not only that, there would be talk, a need for explanations. It was a small town, and everyone knew everyone's business. Monday had been a wash-out, a sick as a dog, lying on the floor, crawling back into bed and shutting out the world kind of day.

Today, she'd felt semi-human, although self-loathing was a bitter pill to swallow. No matter how she tried to justify her decision, there was still the weight of guilt that wouldn't go away. But damn it, she couldn't keep driving in the same rut, day after day! In all of her twenty years in Cordial Creek, nothing exciting had ever happened to her. She was twenty-eight years old, yet she might as well be an old woman with how predictable her days were. Sam had been her everything, and she loved him to pieces, but . . . the routine, the sameness . . . they were wearing thin. This town, its routine and boundaries, held him up and kept him going. Megan didn't see him opening the door to change. Sam was a born-here, live-and-die-here, home-town boy.

He'd never go for a mutual, "Let's see other people, try some other flavors." Sam was old-fashioned; when he gave his heart, he gave it completely and exclusively. She'd been his one and only. Unheard of in today's day and age. If Megan chose to see someone else, that meant breaking it off. Breaking his heart.

She spent the day working on putting herself back into some semblance of order, had just showered and done her nails to get rid of the dirty feeling that she'd done something wrong, when Sam showed up. Now, lying in bed, staring into the darkness and waiting for oblivion that would not come, she should have known better than to think he'd let sleeping dogs lie.

4

Day 1

SAM TOSSED AND turned throughout the night, half awake, half dreaming as his mind worked overtime on the challenge he'd set for himself. Twenty years had passed since Megan first stepped into his life; at thirty, it was most of his lifetime. He had thought their marriage would take place shortly after she finished college. That had been six years ago, something that had been put off too long and now was in danger. He should have done more than talk about it; when she'd been nervous he should have made the proposal, sealed their commitment. Pushed for an answer, one way or another. Maybe she thought he didn't love her enough.

He needed to win back something he never thought he could lose. One thing was certain—he wouldn't give up. O'Malleys were not quitters, and he would not be the first. In the dim light just before dawn, his memories carried him back to the summer when he had first met Meg.

He was 10 years old, she was 8. He was hanging from a tree limb in his backyard when he saw moving trucks at the house next door. The sunlight caught on the hair of the cutest little blonde he'd ever seen and had him tumbling to the ground. He lay there, head spinning, certain he saw those stars circling round like in the cartoons.

The little girl ran over to him, pigtails bouncing, bright eyes of blue opened wide. "Are you okay? That was a long ways down! I'm Megan Taylor, by the way." She reached out and pulled him up with a surprisingly strong arm.

Sam smiled but had to wait a moment to talk. He'd had the wind knocked out of him—from the fall or the girl? When he could breathe again, he held out a hand like he'd seen grown-ups do. "I'm Sam O'Malley. Welcome to the neighborhood."

She winked at him. "Nice to meet ya! We've just come from Washington, D.C. and we're here to stay. Daddy promised! I'm so excited. A real home, and you're the first neighbor I've met. I bet you're good luck. I've gotta go unpack. See ya later!" She skipped away to join her parents in the moving efforts.

Sam spent the rest of the day trying to catch a glimpse of her. He even tried to help unpack, but his mother said he'd be underfoot. That night, Meg's family cooked a barbecue and sat out on their back deck. It was Sam's perfect chance. He popped up the steps with a fist full of red roses and thrust them in Meg's face. "Here's a welcome present!"

Megan took them carefully when she saw his hands were bleeding from the thorns. "Thank you, Sam. They're real pretty, my most favorite flower in the whole world. Where did you get them?"

Sam's mother's voice carried to them from her garden. "Samuel Patrick O'Malley, what did you do to my rose bushes?"

Sam's eyes opened wide. He knew he was in trouble. "I gotta go!" He scampered home.

Sam's eyes opened as he came back to the present. He sat up in bed. He knew what he needed to do. He showered, dressed, and headed into town. He'd go to a store this time around.

MEGAN STUMBLED down the stairs and put on water for tea. It had been a rough night, with Sam's visit looping continuously in her mind with no way to change the ending. To top it off, when she did fall asleep, she dreamed. Her dreams carried her back to that day she met Sam, except this time, when he fell out of the tree, it killed him. *My fault! It's all my fault!* Heart pounding and face wet with tears, Megan shot out of bed and began to pace.

That day, when they moved in next to the O'Malleys . . . it had been the eighth house she'd lived in over a period of eight years. Her father had been in the service. They went from base to base annually, pulling up stakes like the circus that traveled through town. No attachments, no family, no gatherings for holidays. An army brat.

The morning of the move, she had hunkered down in the corner of her attic bedroom, determined not to go. Tears streaked down her face, and she didn't bother to wipe them away. She pressed her forehead to her knees and wished she had a dog to keep her company when her family left. They couldn't have a dog, not when all they ever did was move.

"Sweet Pea, it's time. Mommy's waiting in the car." Her father's step was heavy, crossing the hardwood floor that creaked. He was tired. Tired of the chore of moving, tired of the fight to rally his family together. Megan could see it in his face. He dropped down next to her and put an arm around her shoulders.

She pulled away. "I'm not going. No more moving. I hate it, Daddy! I never have any real friends because I have to let them all go! I never get to have a favorite spot or a place of my own. I'm staying here! I'll ask the people if I can live here. Maybe I can be their maid like 'The Little Princess.' Remember that movie with Shirley Temple?"

Her father almost laughed, thought better of it when he saw the stubborn set to his daughter's jaw. He knew that stubbornness; he'd seen it in the mirror.

"Meggie, I promise you this is the last time we move. Mommy feels just like you do. She's had enough. No more being in the service, no more pulling up stakes, and we'll stay put. Please come downstairs. Your mother will never forgive me if I let you be a servant girl."

In the end, Megan went with them. Of course she did; she was eight, an only child, and she had to go. What if there had been a brother or sister? Maybe they would have forgotten about her then. She imagined that story for the drive. They drove for hours, from southern Pennsylvania up to Vermont, and the green of the mountains had her pressing her face to the window, the blue of the lakes catching her breath. Beautiful, she thought she'd never seen anything more beautiful until they drove down a quiet, country road to a little white house with a picket fence and sunflowers tilting their faces to the sky like out of a fairy tale. But the most beautiful thing of all was the boy next door with chocolate eyes, sun-bleached hair, all tall and stretched out. When he fell out of that tree branch, Sam O'Malley fell into Meg's life.

Cordial Creek was her first permanent residence when her father took a teaching job at the military academy. And Sam . . . he'd been her first real friend. Growing roots, blooming where she was planted, having someone she could call her own . . . it had been a real comfort to her . . . at first.

But year after year, nothing changed, and inside she grew restless, unsettled, dissatisfied. Chalk it up to all those moves early on; maybe Daddy's career and feeling like she lived out of a suitcase had soured her on staying in any one place for too long.

The sunlight hurt eyes that were puffy and red from crying when Megan opened her front door to get her morning newspaper early on Wednesday morning.

Blonde hair tumbling out of a ponytail and drifting into her eyes, she brushed it away to clear her line of vision. Resting on top of the paper was a bouquet of red roses cushioned with Baby's Breath and greens. She gathered them into her arms, went inside, and opened the card with trembling fingers.

Dear Meg,

20 blossoms, one for each year that we've spent together. I chose your most favorite flower in the world. I learned that on the first day I met you.

Sam

P.S. Don't worry—I didn't steal them this time. My mother would still kick my butt.

Megan pressed the flowers close to her face and inhaled their scent, remembering the flowers from that first day. Sam's mother had been furious. Megan felt so terrible, she even brought them over and offered to return them, but Mrs. O'Malley was too gracious to take back a gift that had been given, no matter how misguided. It was a wonder Sam was ever allowed to see her again after that fiasco.

He made her love roses even more that day. He'd given her more, many times and in many colors over the years. Helped her to put in the bushes around her home, made them flourish because he had a green thumb like his mother. She walked back inside and placed them in a vase on her kitchen table. They'd be the first thing she saw each morning before leaving for work and each evening when she came home.

SAM MADE IT to work at his usual time, ahead of Michael. He went back to inspect the damages he had caused and was pleased to see not only had it been repaired but improvements had been made in the design to justify a change. He strode back to his office to review plans for the day and his agenda. When Michael wandered in a half hour later, sucking down coffee like it should be intravenous, Sam was working high above on the beams that formed the skeleton of the building. Michael didn't like heights or Sam's choice of starting the day at his present location, but there was no help for it. He'd have to join the boss to have a conversation.

"What are you doing up here without a hard hat?" Michael called out as he cautiously performed a balancing act to reach his friend. He felt like a tightrope walker, wavering slightly to the left and right but finally steadied and dropped down to straddle the beam. He set a hard hat on Sam's head and stared glumly into his empty coffee cup. Here one moment, gone the next.

Sam grinned at him through the screws he held between his teeth. "I forgot. Had my mind on other things. It's not like that thing would help me if I fell anyway."

Michael glanced down uncomfortably, his stomach dropping as he took in the distance to the ground. "You're not . . . intentionally falling isn't one of the things on your mind, is it?"

Sam stopped what he was doing, set everything down so he could give his complete attention to his best friend. "I have never and will never think about such a thing. Got it? Now get to work."

Pure relief washed over Michael as he saw and heard the truth in Sam's clear eyes. "You bet, Boss."

SAM KICKED OFF his work boots when there was a knock at the door immediately followed by Michael's entrance. He carried a pizza in one arm, a six pack of beer in the other. Both found a place on the counter along with Michael as he hoisted himself up and popped a can open. He tossed another to Sam before grabbing a piece of pepperoni pizza that was oozing with grease and cheese. "Mmm . . . perfect."

"I'm glad you feel so comfortable here," Sam teased, taking his own food out to the living room. He sat on the couch, leaned back, and rested his feet on the coffee table before taking a long sip of his cold drink.

Michael joined him, and they sat quietly for a while until he suddenly slammed his can down in frustration. Sam jerked and almost spilled his beer down his shirt. "All right! I can't stand it! Spill it, O'Malley! What's going on with you? You don't come to work, then you're a human wrecking ball and a wreck, then you're okay. You've got my head spinning so I don't know which way's up. Are you in some kind of trouble?"

Sam laid a reassuring hand on Michael's shoulder, his voice steady enough to calm the thunderheads in his friend's eyes. "There's nothing to tell. Check in with me at the end of the month. I might be able to give you the details then. Right now, it's status quo."

MEGAN DUCKED into the bookstore next to the pizza place on Main Street when she saw Michael Flannigan heading in. The last thing she needed was to face Sam's best friend. The three of them had been involved in many scrapes, adventures, and bouts of mischief since her arrival; they'd been dubbed the three musketeers by their parents.

The knot in her stomach gave a good twist; it had

formed the moment she got out of Sam's car and walked to the cab. It wasn't going away, and she knew—if Michael found out what she did, he'd give it a good yank, maybe add a few more. Loyal was the best way to describe him and hard-headed. He'd defend Sam first, figure out the facts later.

Hovering by the window with a book hiding half of her face, Megan watched Michael's retreating figure climb into his beater truck and take off. Old Faithful was his nickname for it, another fitting comparison to the man. That she couldn't face him was another indicator of her guilt. It was wrong, what she had done to Sam. There was no talking her way out of the fact, even to herself.

Cursing under her breath and miserable to boot, she walked out of the shop and slipped into the driver's seat of her own car. Her intention had been to get a pizza; usually, she'd be having something with Sam. Thanks to her brilliant decision making and the sight of Michael, her empty stomach wasn't getting anything. *Good job, Meg. Things are really looking up.*

Leaning back with her head against the head rest, she decided there was only one cure: girl talk. It had to be someone who understood her, had been through her own ups and downs. Picking up her cell phone, Megan pressed the speed dial button, waited, let out her breath in relief when Sophie answered. "Sophie, can I come over? I need you." Say no more.

They sat on the back porch of the second floor; the living quarters were upstairs while the business took up the bottom floor of the old farmhouse. Sophia Carmella Farriello, originally of Brooklyn, always carried the city with her in her heart; after college, she opened "Eye Candy," a shop that focused on beauty products, jewelry, gifts, and a salon to pamper a woman. It catered to the feminine side of life and fulfilled the craving for the big city without ever having to leave the "backyard" down home.

Sophie had just finished giving Megan the full treatment—shampoo and conditioner, nails, a facial—and topped it off with appletinis. They leaned back on a chaise lounge and watched the moonlight falling on the gardens below. Sophie twisted a curl of red hair around her finger and tipped her head toward her best friend; usually smiling, Megan had a worry line marring her smooth forehead, and her eyes stared out, unseeing. "So, are you ready to tell me what's bothering you? You've turned down my cannolis—a first—and you haven't given a bit of dish when there's usually some juicy tidbit from the law office. What gives?"

Megan couldn't tell Sophie about Sam, or she'd be checked into the asylum. Sophie loved Sam; everyone in Cordial Creek loved Sam. He was everything good wrapped in one package and then some. Megan blew hair out of her eyes and swallowed her drink fast. Her best friend's green eyes grew wide, but she poured another and cleared her throat encouragingly. "Nothing. Nothing I can put my finger on. It's just . . . everything is always the same. I feel like I'm waiting for something to happen. What if it never does?"

"Meggie, we all feel that way sometimes. Maybe you need a vacation or a little trip. We could go into the city on the weekend, go to the shops, watch a show. What do you say?" Sophie was the best tour guide when they went into the Big Apple; she knew all the ins and outs.

Go? She couldn't go now. Sam had asked for twenty days; if Megan left, he'd think it was over. Something inside of her didn't want that finality, not yet, was holding on even though she started this train wreck. "No, I can't. There's too much going on at work, and

Sam might want to do something."

Sophie poured another drink and patted Meg's hand. "Waiting to see what Sam is up to is not a bad thing."

Day 2

MEGAN DIDN'T find anything new from Sam when she woke up. She was disappointed even though she had no justification to feel that way; maybe he was completely disgusted with her. She pawed through hangers in her closet, yanking one thing out then another, but dissatisfied with everything. Nothing looked right, nothing fit right; the real problem: the state of her mind.

The absence of a memento from Sam gnawed at her all day long. Perhaps he'd given up after one day, considered it a lost cause, and turned to E-LoveMe. The dating website would probably find him someone more desirable and compatible, proving he'd been a fool to spend his life on the likes of her.

Her anxious doubt was like a splinter under her skin at the law office where she'd been a paralegal for the past six years. She became increasingly cranky with little toleration for others and thought she'd scream if she had to sift through one more hefty law document. Once again she berated herself for not becoming a lawyer so she could reap the benefits of another paralegal's hard work. Her co-workers felt the bite of her tongue, the heat of her glare, and kept their distance.

The mood didn't help her attitude about her job. Funny thing about her job—it wasn't her first choice. What she really dreamed of being was a writer of children's books. She loved to write, draw, paint pictures with her mind. English and art class had been her favorites. But when it was time to choose a career, her father had told her to be practical; writing might not ever pan out.

What did she choose? Something with no imagination. The job of a paralegal was cut and dried, black and white. At least lawyers had the art of the argument; that required some creativity. But if she was honest with herself, she didn't want to be a lawyer, either. Safe and stable, that had been her choice, and it, too, made her feel trapped.

By the time Megan pulled into her driveway at the end of the day, she was an absolute bear. She slammed her car door and stomped up the front steps. A heel broke on one of her shoes in response and had her steaming even more, until she saw the basket. It sat on her top step, white wicker to match her porch furniture. Inside was something in blue tissue paper. He'd chosen her favorite color. Coincidence? Not when it came to Sam. Megan reached in and found an assortment of all of her favorite chocolates nestled inside with a note.

> *Dear Meg,*
>
> *I know you keep a secret hoard for times when you are stressed, upset, a little blue. Haven't you heard? All's fair in love and chocolate.*
>
> *Sam*

She dropped down on the step, slipped the other shoe off of her aching foot, and pulled her hair out of its neat bun. She picked one bar of chocolate and took a bite, enjoying a taste of heaven. Her eyes darted left to right, scanning the area. There was no sign of Sam. She took another bite and closed her eyes, seeing her childhood bedroom once again.

It was the first day of middle school, and Megan was flung across her bed, sobbing her eyes out into her pillow. Sam was next to her, rubbing her back, saying comforting things, and just being Sam. He was always there for her. When everything in life felt topsy-turvy, Sam was the one thing that was right side up.

Talk about topsy-turvy. That first day had been hell! Nothing made sense in that terrible time. Emotions were running haywire. She felt uncomfortable in her own skin and absolutely ugly. She didn't fit in anywhere.

"Come on, tell me what happened. It can't be that bad," Sam soothed. He'd been trying to get her to confide in him ever since the bus stopped at the middle school. He had started ninth grade at the high school that day, and it had been no picnic. He was at the bottom of the pond with much bigger fish at the top. However, it wasn't time for his problems. Megan had been crying the minute she stepped off the bus. He held her all the way home, his heart pounding and anger building. If someone had caused this, Sam would make him or her pay. He squeezed her shoulder. "Come on, Meggie, please tell me. What happened?"

Megan rolled over and stared up at her best friend in the world. His coffee-colored eyes, sweet as chocolate drops, were troubled, filled with concern for her. Why couldn't all of those middle school brats be like him? She sniffled and rubbed at red, bloodshot eyes. "They called me four eyes and metal mouth! Somebody called me an ugly dog and barked!" It was supposed to be easier, going to a new school. She'd lived in Cordial Creek for nearly five years, made friends. The boys . . . they were expected to be idiots, but the girls? Some of them had hung out with her, but today they cut her down, made fun of her clothes, avoided her at lunch. Mean. They could be so mean.

Sam clenched his teeth for a moment. It took an effort to relax. "Well, it's because they're jealous of you if they're girls and they like you if they're boys. I know it sounds messed up, but it's true." He smiled and hugged her, hoping she'd believe him because he knew what he was talking about. Her glasses made her cuter than ever, and so what about braces? Sam knew that in a few years Megan would blow all the rest out of the water, and he couldn't wait to see it. He planned on being the only one by her side, just like now.

Megan giggled a little, her breath a hiccup from crying. "You really think so? You're not just saying that?"

Sam gave her another hug. It was a brotherly hug because that was all she was ready for, and he would be whatever she needed, whenever she needed it. "I'm positive! I'm a guy, remember? We talk about this stuff."

They sat quietly for a moment and then Megan sprang up and rummaged through her dresser drawer until she returned with a chocolate bar. "You want some?" She popped a piece in her mouth.

Sam accepted, his smile growing until it stretched across his face, and he poked her in the ribs. "Still under your pajamas, huh? How much you got in there in case I need a loan? My day wasn't so hot either."

Megan turned her attention to his problems, and then they laughed together as he told her about his day, managing to turn everything into something funny. Somehow, Sam managed to make light of her troubles as well, as he always did.

Their laughter echoed in Meg's mind as she opened her eyes, still sitting on her step as the sun began to set. Sam always knew what she needed. She stood up and walked inside, heading to her bedroom. The new supply of chocolate was added to the rest, in her dresser drawer, under her pajamas. She set the basket on her night stand with her notes from Sam in the bottom. What would tomorrow bring?

Anticipation tingled inside of her. She'd said she was looking for a change in her life. She hadn't bargained for Sam, Mr. Same Ol' Same Ol', to take her by surprise in this way. She now had something to look forward to in each new day as he brought her a piece of herself and their past. She couldn't help but wish she was a kid again, stretched out on her bed with her best friend, sharing a piece of chocolate.

5

Day 3

SAM COULDN'T sleep . . . again. Ever since Megan had decided to turn his world upside down, his mind had been on overdrive; at first, he'd been trying to wrap himself around the concept of life without her, then was consumed with how he could keep her in it. Even when he was occupied at work, speaking to clients, or hanging out with Michael, his subconscious worked on all of the little things that mattered about Meg.

The clock numbers glowed brightly, announcing it was three in the morning. Way too early to be awake. He stared, wide-eyed, at the ceiling. He was stumped about what to bring her next. Unable to lie still any longer and hopeful that motion would help, Sam pulled on running pants and a sweatshirt. He slipped out of the house and started to jog on the back country roads that surrounded his house. It was dark and quiet; everything still slept.

The air was cool on this early autumn night on the outskirts of Cordial Creek. The stars and the moon provided the only light; there would be no street lights until he reached the small town. Light wasn't necessary. He knew these roads with his eyes closed. He'd spent his whole life here. He loved being surrounded by mountains, lakes, forest, and the country. It was a short distance from town to any kind of getaway a person could want.

Sam had never wanted to go elsewhere. His four years away in college were simply something to be endured as he attended the best school of architecture, one that prepared him to give something back to his community. Most of his friends thought he was insane. Even Michael had left for a few years after college, until home and a lucrative job offer as Sam's partner, brought him back.

For Sam, his town was everything. It was part of his very fabric. It was the mom-and-pop store on the corner, where he bought candy as a child and the best fresh cuts of meat as an adult. It was Mabel at the post office, like a grandmother to him; she often brought fresh cookies to send home. It was Gina at the diner, who poured his coffee just the way he liked it and knew what he wanted to eat before he did. It was the school yard filled with children, where his initials could still be seen on a playground picnic table. It was the little white church where his parents had been married and he'd been baptized. It was the cemetery next to the church where his ancestors, his grandparents, and his father slept. It was the one place where he felt grounded. In this crazy world where nothing stayed the same, his memories would always be cradled here, be a definite constant in his life.

Sam's feet carried him several miles by their own will until he found himself at his father's grave. He paced back and forth, bringing down his heart rate until it would allow him to sit in front of a stone cross. He kissed his fingers and pressed them to his father's name, James O'Malley. Time to be patient; something he'd learned to do in this place. Gradually, a feeling of peace settled over him. Sam knew his father was not here anymore; however, there was his presence, a nearness, that wasn't felt anywhere else. "Thanks, Dad," he said in a hushed voice, unwilling to break the calm that surrounded him. "I'm sure you know why I'm here. Am I doing the right thing, trying to keep her? Or should I let her go? And if I let her go, what then? There's only been Meg, always Meg, since day one."

Sam closed his eyes and waited. He'd learned about waiting for what he wanted in life. He'd waited to grow older, to find love, to figure out what he would be. The hardest wait had been for healing after he lost his dad. His patience paid off yet again as the air shifted slightly around him. A sensation of warmth that could only be his father's love washed over him. In his mind, he heard his dad's advice from years ago. *Follow your heart. It's the only thing you can ever do.*

Sam nodded and brushed at cheeks that had become wet. It was a powerful experience whenever he came here, filling him with emotions that could not be contained. "I'll try, Dad and . . . I love you, too."

He took his time on the return run home, more at peace with himself. He should've gone to Dad sooner. He knew what to bring Megan next.

MEGAN OPENED her eyes before the alarm went off. The sun was peeping through the windows, on its way up for the day. She pulled the covers over her head and waited to face the morning; she hated mornings, had to psych herself up. When she tried again, something shiny caught her eye. Hanging on a branch outside her window, a package wrapped in gold paper swayed in the wind. Megan threw back the covers and tiptoed to the window. What had Sam been up to now? To what extremes would he go next?

She opened the window, the crisp air making her shiver as she reached out to grab her package. She closed the window quickly and ran back to bed like a child with a Christmas present. Wrapping herself in a cocoon of covers before opening the box, she held it tightly, eyes squeezed shut. Pulling on the wrapping, fingers feeling the way, she opened her eyes wide. Her smile stretched as she took out a tiny, glass figure. It was small enough to rest in the palm of her hand and be completely hidden when she closed her fingers. A miniature robin with a fiery red breast and bright eyes stared back at her. In the box was a note.

> *Dear Meg,*
>
> *Do you remember Ruby, our baby bird? You found him, and you were so determined, come hell or high water, that you would save him. I didn't think it could be done, but as in all things concerning you, that didn't matter. I had to help. We went to the library, we called the vet, and we rigged up a homemade incubator in your attic because it was the warmest place we could think of. We're lucky we didn't burn down the house! Every day, we took turns feeding him, giving him water, holding him, and loving him. And because you wouldn't give up, he made it. I remember how you cried when it was time to let him go. You loved Ruby so much, the way he'd come to you, how he'd sing, the little marking on his wing like a white starburst. You knew he had to go because he was meant to be free. I'll never forget how you were about to burst with happiness when Ruby came back every*

day to the tree outside your window. He made a nest and kept coming back, and then his babies came next.

I give you this little Ruby because I love you enough to set you free. But, like our Ruby, I hope my love will be enough to make you come back to me. You've always been free with me, free to show every part of yourself and be you without being afraid of what I'll think.

Sam

The tears were brimming as Megan held the figure up to the sun, making the red glow and the small facets of light dance on the wall. She gave the tiny bird a kiss and set it on her windowsill for a daily reminder of Ruby . . . and, she had to admit, Sam.

The little bird was a painful reminder of one other fact: it was symbolic of taking flight, being free. To see the world, go to new places, do the unexpected. Sam was a good ol' hometown boy; he'd be pleased as punch to be parked in a rocker when he was an old man, watching the dust settle in the road and thinking of bygone days. Leaving Cordial Creek would be as foreign to him as a fish planning a trip across land. It would suck him dry, make it so he couldn't breathe.

Exactly the way Megan felt by staying put.

6

Day 4

SAM SAT AT the counter at the Cordial Creek Diner on his lunch break. He sipped Gina's coffee, the best in town, with two sugars and heavy on the cream, "Almost as sweet as you, honey," she said. "Now, you want a little coffee with the rest of what's in that cup?" She said the same thing every time she served him, always with a wink. His turkey with Swiss on rye bread—Gina told him that's what he wanted—sat untouched as he stared at the local newspaper, only pretending to read.

"Carry me piggyback, Sammy! The floor's cold, and I hate to walk around without any slippers!" It was the first of many innocent sleepovers. Their families were already accustomed to seeing an extra face at the table; if their child wasn't home, they knew where to find him or her. The strong bond between Megan and Sam had forged a friendship for their parents as well.

This first sleepover at Sam's was also Megan's first time away from her family. She was trying to be brave, but she felt homesick. How silly it seemed now, when she could see the light shining in her parents' bedroom next door.

Sam played along, scooping Megan onto his back, and galloped through the house until they were laughing. She soon forgot the upset feeling in her stomach. He tossed her on the bottom bunk bed and returned a moment later with slipper socks in his hand. "Here, Meggie. You can wear these. Maime gave 'em to me for Christmas, and I haven't worn 'em yet. They'll keep your feet nice

*and toasty." He climbed up to the top bunk and turned out the light.
He lay back with his arms behind his head and a big grin, content
to know his best friend would be there all night and in the morning.*

*A quiet sniffling had him hanging his head over the side,
trying to see in the dim glow of his night light. "Meggie, are you
okay?"*

*"I'm scared, Sammy. I want to go home," she wailed in a
small voice.*

*Sam swung down next to her, "Scoot over. I'll keep you
company. It'll be okay." He snuggled in close and put his arm
around her, better than any teddy bear. It didn't take long for either
one to fall asleep. Every time Megan stayed at Sam's, she wore his
slippers; many times he'd end up in the bottom bunk with her. Still
just eight and ten years old, they couldn't imagine anything improper
about that.*

"You're insultin' Joe if you don't start making a dent
in that sandwich," Gina said. She nudged Sam's arm in a
good-natured way. "Where's your mind at, anyway? You
look like you're a thousand miles away." Gina was
plump and motherly, always clucking over Sam to try
and brighten his day. She wore her hair up in a ponytail,
her makeup just-so, and her t-shirts bore cheerful
slogans.

Sam dipped his head in embarrassment and took a
bite of his lunch. More like twenty *years* away. "Tell Joe
this is really good. I'll take a piece of chocolate cream
pie, too."

"That's more like it. You're looking a little thinner
than I'd like to see, Mr. O'Malley." She bustled away to
take care of his request and her other customers.

The pie arrived soon after with a tall glass of
milk—"I know what my boy likes," per Gina—giving
Sam the chance to really enjoy it.

Because by then he'd solved the daily puzzle of
what to bring Megan.

MEGAN FOUND her next gift in the evening, tucked in with her mail when she came home from work. The mail was set aside, unopened on the table, as she slipped out of her jacket and pulled down her ponytail. She put her feet up with a sigh on the chair across from her and opened her latest package. It was an old pair of blue slippers that had been mended and patched many times. They were soft on her cheek. She plucked the note out of one.

> *Dear Meg,*
>
> *Do you remember Maime's slipper socks? You borrowed them on your first sleepover at my house and wore them a thousand times after. At first they were so big they swallowed your feet, but you grew into them. I saved them because they make me think of you. When I went to college, I took them with me—stuck them in the back of an old tote bag in my dorm closet. I don't want to sound weird, but they reminded me of you and home.*
>
> > *Sam*

Megan slipped them on and didn't take them off. Dinner was a lonely affair, sitting on the couch with the TV for company even though she barely noticed what was on the screen. Her head was filled with Sam, the flood of memories washing over her.

Bedtime was even worse. He had always called her to say goodnight; another tradition. A routine she found she missed now that it hadn't happened since her self–imposed exile. She climbed into bed, slippers still on her feet. Her dreams carried her back to a bottom bunk, her best friend, when everything was right in the world. She remembered the years when Sam was away at college. The sense that he'd taken a piece of her with him. When had she stopped feeling that way about him?

7

Day 5

MEGAN STUMBLED down to the kitchen, wiping sleep from her eyes. It was Sunday morning, and she'd slept in until she felt like a zombie. She set the tea kettle on to boil and opened the door to find a large bundle of newspaper comics tied with a bow. No matter how much the world changed, with newspapers going out of business and everyone switching to their smartphones and tablets, Sam knew how much she loved reading the old-fashioned comics.

> *Dear Meg,*
> *Think of how many Sundays we spent*
> *under a throw blanket on the sofa,*
> *drinking in coffee, tea, each other.*
>
> *Sam*

She made a cup of tea and took his advice. Or tried to.

"SAMMY, MY friend, this was a great idea!" Michael sighed in contentment as he stretched out in the rowboat and propped his head on a life preserver. The air was refreshing, the fish were biting, and the beer was cold. He couldn't ask for anything more.

Sam, equally lazy, mirrored the picture of relaxation at the opposite end of the boat. The sun beat down on his bare head, making it feel more like summer. They'd been out on the water since dawn. Once the noon hour hit, they started working on the cooler of beer and easily worked their way through a six pack. Sam opened a new can, making a dent on another pack.

"So, Sam, what's Megan up to? I haven't seen her lately," Michael asked in what he hoped was an off-hand way. He suspected she was the cause of the melt down a week ago but was not about to admit it.

Sam feigned a grin and nudged Michael's leg with his boot. "Smooth, but I know what you're up to. If I know my Meg—and I do—she's having a slow, easy day just like ours. She's probably in bed, reading the comics and snoozing. Anything else you want to know?"

"Can you toss me another beer?" Michael asked, hand up and ready to catch as Sam sent one over. He popped the top and took a good, long swallow. Sam was suddenly up on his feet.

"I've got something big!" He grabbed his pole. Something tugged hard enough that he almost lost his rod.

Michael sat up and held on to the sides of the boat as it started to rock. "Whoa, Sammy, just watch it! You're going to—" He never had a chance to finish. Next thing they knew, they were both in the lake along with the poles, tackle boxes, and . . . "Not the beer! Save the beer!" Michael called as he dove down into the chilly water. Sam scrambled to salvage what he thought was more important—the gear.

A half hour later, they sat shivering in front of Sam's fire place, wearing sweatpants and t-shirts while their clothes were in the dryer. "It was a little nippy out there. Sorry about that," Sam told his best friend. He sighed deeply as the heat began to seep in. "You have to admit we did have an adventure."

Michael raised an eyebrow as he burned his tongue on a cup of hot chocolate. "Yeah, it was an adventure. Never a dull moment with you, O'Malley. So, tell me, why are you sitting here with my soggy, ugly self instead of spending the afternoon with Meg?"

Sam took the easy way out and decided to lie. "I called her. She's coming down with a cold, she thinks. Said to feed you a steak and come by later, after she's had a long nap."

"All right, I accept that dinner invitation."

Steaks, a football game, and more beer followed. Michael stood up and staggered. "Whoops. There. Okay. I'm fine. Well, morning is going to get here awfully early. I'd better head out."

Sam clapped a hand on his shoulder and steered him away from the door. "Hit the spare room. I'll see you in the morning."

"You goin' to see Megan now? Say hi to her for me. G'night."

"Goodnight."

Michael wandered to the spare bedroom, frowning. Meg's absence that evening left a gap that the two men kept avoiding. Wherever Sam was, that was where Megan should be, too. However, Sam had closed the subject. Perhaps Michael should go see Megan tomorrow . . . or maybe he'd just stay the hell out of it and mind his own business. He knew the saying, "Curiosity killed the cat." This was one cat that was not being cheated out of one of his lives over trouble in paradise. "'Night, Sam," he called out with bleary friendship, then climbed atop the guest bed and fell asleep.

MEGAN SPENT THE entire day attempting to enjoy being sinfully lazy. She started with the comics, moved on to a nap, and finished with ice cream and a movie in bed. And missed Sam, terribly. Lazy days were perfect, but only when there was someone sharing them. Sam.

When she closed her eyes that night, she felt unsettled. None of it felt right; wrong, it was all wrong. Of course . . . because Sam wasn't there. Like a photograph with half of the scene cut out, like the time her mother had broken up with a disastrous boyfriend then cut him out of every picture. When asked why she kept her half, Mom had answered, "Because I looked damned good."

The problem: Sam was no disaster. Megan was.

SAM PICKED UP the few dishes and beer bottles, locked up, and headed to bed. His head was spinning. He stretched out and closed his eyes. It dawned on him that life never stopped, not for broken hearts, not for grief, not for regret. There would be no more hanging in limbo as he awaited the outcome. There was no time to waste; his father's death had taught him that lesson. He had to make sure he lived each minute while he was in it. He had no idea what he should do next. Each new day was all he had, and he had to make good use of it. There was no denying one fact: he hated every minute without Meg.

8

Day 6

SAM HAD FORGOTTEN how bad even a beer hangover could hurt. He ignored the headache as best he could and headed to work.

That day was a blur. The sun pricked at Sam's eyelids with exceeding brightness, prompting him to dig out his sunglasses. No one else wore them that day except for Michael, who grimly nodded to him with sympathy whenever they crossed paths. The noise on the job site thundered in Sam's brain with incessant volume, resulting in a retreat to his office. Every call that came in turned out to be a hassle, adding to what promised to be the granddaddy of all headaches. Everything seemed to be conspiring against him. Just when he thought he couldn't take it any longer, the end of the day arrived. Sam headed home rather than stay late as was customary. He waved to Michael, who looked equally miserable, as he drove away.

Sam made one brief stop, dropped a gift at Megan's, then continued home. He somehow managed to hit every bump in the road, until he thought his head would explode. Once inside, he dosed himself with an over-the-counter pain med, drew the blinds, and hit the bed. He didn't even have the energy to take off his clothes. Never again would he drink that much beer at one time. He was too old for this crap. Missing Megan added to the sensation that his entire world was full of pain.

MEG'S DAY HAD gone well, but only in anticipation of Sam's next surprise. Her heart lifted at the sight of her newest mystery present, hanging on the knob of her front door. She stood on her stoop in the evening chill, opened a large gift bag decorated with snowflakes, and pulled out a fleece blanket. She held it close. It felt as soft as she once imagined a cloud would be when she was a child. A cheerful snowman smiled back at her when she unfolded it, begging to be snuggled.

She went inside, changed into comfy clothes, and made herself a cup of tea. Once she was wrapped up in her blanket, feet tucked beneath her, then she could give her attention to her note. It was like the days of old, when girls were courted. She could picture Sam fitting in perfectly in that older, simpler time, arriving with his horse and buggy. He would be wearing a suit, dashing and dapper, a catch envied by all, bearing gifts and sending her love letters like the one she held in her hand.

> *Dear Meg,*
>
> *It was the first frost this morning. Bed and my warm blankets called to me and almost won. It made me think of you, how you're always cold and can't sleep without a blanket. You always tell me I'm your heater.*
>
> *Sam*
>
> *P.S. Doesn't the snowman on the blanket remind you of Frankie?*

Megan searched through her large collection of photo albums. She was a photo fanatic. She flipped through picture after picture until she found a picture of Frankie the Snowman. Did Sam forget nothing? She peered closely at the rosy-cheeked girl and tall, gangly boy who stood next to a towering snowman. Megan could feel the temperature drop and see the woods where Frankie came to life.

"He's perfect, Sammy, just like Frosty. Your daddy's hat is perfect. Will he miss it?" Megan asked eagerly, whirling around just in time to miss a snowball aimed at her head.

"Nah—it's an old one. He never wears it." Sam threw another snowball, making his mark this time. A full-fledged war ensued until they were on the ground with Sam pinning Megan down. He was twelve-years-old and had hit a growth spurt. There was no way Megan could throw him off. "Beg for mercy!"

Megan angrily banged on his chest with her mittens. "Samuel O'Malley, you get off of me this instant or I'll . . . I'll bite you!"

Sam laughed at her ferocious expression and rolled off of her. "You look just like the cowardly lion in The Wizard of Oz!*"*

Megan stood up and marched in the direction of home, her chin and nose pointed up to the sky. She was in a full huff. Sam grabbed the snowman's hat and placed it on his head at a funny angle. He caught up to Megan easily with his big, loping steps. "Come on, Meggie! Don't be mad! I'll let you throw one in my face."

It was too good of an opportunity to be passed up. Megan landed one right between Sam's eyes. He made sure to be extra dramatic before he toppled over. Megan stretched out in the snow next to him, and they made snow angels. Tired of that, Megan snatched the hat and placed it back on the snowman's head. She studied him closely and nodded with inspiration. "He reminds me of Frank Sinatra, you know? When he was young and dashing in those old movies our mothers watch together. Let's call him Frankie."

Sam stood next to her and squeezed her hand. "Frankie . . .

I like it. I wish he could come to life like Frosty."

Megan turned and gave Sam a fierce hug. "But he does come to life when you're around, Sammy. You make magic happen."

The grown-up Megan now stared into the bright eyes of herself as a child and took the time to really look into Sam's eyes, too. Even then, she meant the world to him. He could never hide his powerful feelings; to this day, they always showed in his eyes, his soul's windows. Megan closed the album and held it close to her chest. When had she forgotten that Sam was a magician?

The question remained: could he pull happiness out of his hat for the two of them now?

Her doubts and discontent had been brewing for a while. Everything had grown stale, and she didn't know if it was simply something wrong with her. The old saying, "The grass is always greener on the other side," kept playing through her mind. But . . . what if it wasn't? Her determination to leave Cordial Creek, to leave Sam, began to waver.

9

Day 7

SAM'S HEAD STILL ached the next morning as he slapped on a hard hat and strode inside the building where Michael was hanging drywall. He braced himself for what was to come. Michael had tried to win the morning race since he first started working with Sam. He'd be sure to rub in his victory.

Michael didn't even turn around. "Kneel in my great presence, oh late one. Come on, you know the deal." He stood tall, his shoulders straight, eyes closed in sweet anticipation.

"You are the early one. Your mission has been fulfilled. Long may we all remember the day Michael Flannigan made it to work before me."

"You're not off the hook yet. You know what you have to do."

Sam grunted. "Don't get too used to this." Ten minutes later, he returned with a dozen donuts and two large coffees.

The day followed its normal course from that point on. Even though Sam and Michael were partners, Michael preferred being a foreman while Sam was the boss, overseeing all details from the design of a project, beginning to end. Sam was a natural leader, excellent at organization and at dealing with clients. He was the architect but was involved in all aspects of their projects and wasn't afraid to get his hands dirty.

Today, Sam was supervising a crew that was moving slabs of granite to be used for the courtyard. They were just passing under some scaffolding when an urgent voice called, "Heads up!"

Sam didn't have time to think, simply act. He shoved two workers out of the way. A wooden beam came crashing down, glancing off of his hard hat before it smacked him on the shoulder and sent him to the ground.

Michael was at Sam's side within minutes, directing one of the men to call nine-one-one and knocking his own hard hat off of his head in his rush to get an unobstructed view. He knelt down next to Sam and gripped the arm that had not been hit. "Sam! Sammy! Can you hear me?"

"Damn . . . I was just about to get rid of my headache," Sam whispered. "Listen, will you take off my hard hat? It's digging into my skull."

Michael carefully cupped the back of his friend's neck before sliding off his hat. There was a nasty, bruised lump on his right temple. "Just lay still, Sammy. Paramedics are on the way."

Sam shook his head then grimaced at the movement. "I don't need that. Give me a moment, and I'll be fine." To prove his point, he started to sit up.

Michael gently pushed him back down and pressed a hand to his chest. "I don't think so. You're not going anywhere." The sound of sirens announced the arrival of the ambulance and ended any chance at an argument. The paramedics, Joe Driscoll and Pete Markam, were old friends of Sam's since high school. They quickly made their way in with a stretcher and equipment. Michael moved aside, answering Pete's questions while Joe talked to Sam.

"Hey, Sammy. Where are you experiencing any pain?" Joe took Sam's vitals while awaiting an answer.

Sam closed his eyes while he mentally debated which was most pressing—the throbbing headache or the gnawing on his shoulder that radiated down his arm. "My shoulder's killing me, and my head's not far behind."

Pete surveyed the beam lying next to Sam and hefted it. It had to be over fifty pounds; it would be very dangerous coming from such a height. "That was a pretty good hit, Sammy. What about your neck or your back? Does anything else hurt?"

Sam shook his head slightly then clamped his eyes shut as everything began to spin. "No, nothing else."

Joe squeezed his good arm. "Unbelievable. Still tough as a bull and just as stubborn. All right, we won't know the full extent of your injuries until you've had x-rays and an MRI or whatever else they need. We're not taking any chances, so we're going to immobilize your neck and back before we get you to the hospital."

The two men worked together carefully and efficiently, placing Sam on a backboard with a neck brace. They moved him to a stretcher with ease but even that movement caused obvious pain. Sam didn't argue throughout the process, which worried Michael even more; it meant he wasn't shaking this off.

WHAT FELT LIKE hours later, but was more like an hour, a nurse brought Michael in to see Sam. Sam was stretched out on a hospital bed with his eyes closed while his vitals were monitored. The knot on his forehead looked worse, if that was possible, and Sam's shirt had been removed to reveal angry bruising that spread from his shoulder and halfway down his right arm. Michael dragged a chair close to the bed, the legs making an annoying scraping on the floor.

"Hey," Sam said softly, cracking one eye to look at his friend then quickly closing it; the light only aggravated the hammering in his head.

"Hey yourself. I tried to get your mom on the phone but haven't reached her yet. Same with Meg."

Sam forgot himself and shook his head which only made him curse under his breath. "Don't call Megan again. I'll be fine."

"Are you kidding me? Of course I'm calling her."

"Forget that! Damn it!" Sam growled as he sat up in a rush then groaned and held on to his arm. "I'm going to be fine. Don't call anyone. Please." He gritted his teeth until he could trust himself to speak again.

Michael tossed his hands in the air, a stormy expression replacing his regular calm. "You're impossible! All right, I won't call anyone unless the doctor says it's serious. Then all bets are off!"

As if on cue, Doctor Brian Harding, another of their high school friends, walked in with a chart. At any other time, Sam would have been grateful for this additional benefit of a small town; everyone knew each other and took good care of one another. However, right now Sam wasn't thinking very clearly, nor did he want the whole town privy to his accident.

"Hey, Mikey! How are ya, buddy?" Brian slapped his old pal on the back before turning his attention to Sam. He peered down at him over wire-rimmed glasses, looking the part of a hard-working young resident with his disheveled hair and serious manner. "As for our good friend, Sam, not so hot right now, eh?"

Sam cracked his eyes open and gave him the barest hint of a grin. "I've had better days. What's the verdict?"

Brian pulled up a chair and rested his hands on his

knees, eyes intense. "You are a lucky man. If that beam had landed dead center on your head, I don't think you'd still be with us. As it is, you have a mild concussion and extreme bruising down to the bone on your right arm. It's a miracle that nothing is broken. We want you to stay here for another couple of hours for observation. If all is well, you can go home with the orders of rest and pain medication for the shoulder. No work for the rest of the week and no strenuous lifting. If you have any dizziness or fainting spells, do not 'pass Go.' Come directly back here to the ER. Got it?"

In answer, Sam closed his eyes and gave a grunt. *I wish Megan were here. I should call her.*

No. I'm not playing that card. She'd come because she feels sorry for me.

He let his eyes droop shut as Michael left, only to have a nurse tap gently on his arm. "Don't snooze on me, Sam. You need to stay awake while we observe you because of your concussion."

Sam winced at the bright sunlight streaming in. "It's just that the light is really hurting my head. It's hard to keep my eyes open."

In response, the nurse closed the blinds and turned off the lights, leaving one dim light over the counter. "Better? Rest now, but don't fall asleep on me."

Easier said than done. Each time he closed his eyes, he nearly drifted off until the nurse would return again. He was nearing the end of the observation period when a commotion down the hall jerked him awake.

"Katie, get back here! Katie, come back this instant!" A male voice called out. He was trying to be quiet in respect to the patients but getting louder by the second.

The sound of rapidly approaching tiny footsteps approached. A little blonde girl, pony tail bopping on her head, scampered into Sam's room and came to an abrupt halt at the sight of him. Her blue eyes opened wide in innocence. "Hey, Mister! I'm Katie. Who are you? Daddy says I can't talk to strangers, but if I know your name then you're not a stranger. What's your name?"

"Katie, stop bothering people!" A tall, frazzled man strode into the cubicle. He grabbed Katie's hand and waved apologetically to Sam. "I am so sorry. We're on our way to see my wife and Katie's new baby brother. She thought this was the way to their room."

Sam smiled. The little girl reminded him so much of Megan as a kid. "It's okay . . . my name's Sam. A new baby brother is waiting? That's really exciting. You'd better get going so you can be a good big sister." He closed his eyes.

A feather touch brushed his hand, making him shift his right arm slightly and wince. He opened his eyes again to see Katie's small hand resting on his own. "You have a boo-boo. Here. You need this teddy to make you feel better." She glanced back at her father with pleading eyes and a pitiful pout. "We can get another one from the gift shop, right, Daddy? Sam really needs this one."

Her father rested his hand gently on her sunny hair and spoke softly. "Yes, sweetie. That's fine. Now please, let Sam rest." Sam started to protest but his accidental visitor refused. "Please keep it. It will make her happy, and I don't have the energy to argue with her right now."

Sam squeezed Katie's hand. "Thanks, honey. Don't keep your mommy and your baby brother waiting, okay?"

After they left, Sam lay there thinking about the children he'd always expected to have with Meg.

IT WAS GOOD TO be back home.

"Thanks, Michael, for everything. I'll be okay once I rest for a while. Give me a call in the morning."

"Dammit, at least let me call your mother."

"No."

"Awright. Awright. Hold on, you need these pain pills." He brought Sam a glass of water and made sure he took two before leaving the bottle beside the bed. "Anything else?"

Sam was already starting to fade. "No," he mumbled. "I don't need a babysitter. I'll call if I'm in trouble. Don't bother Mom. She doesn't need any more worries. I'll see you tomorrow."

Michael muttered and stomped out. Sam was vaguely aware of the sound of his truck pulling away, as sleep closed in. Then he remembered—Megan's present. He sat up with a not-so-quiet groan and glanced at the clock. He had about an hour before she'd be home from work. He stood up slowly, went to the kitchen, peeled a piece of note paper off a pad, and set it on the table. He sat down, suddenly dizzy. He blamed it on the medicine.

Now came the hard part. He clenched his jaw and lifted his right arm onto the table with his left hand. Why couldn't he be a leftie? Even that little bit of movement had him sweating with pain. He picked up a pen and wrote a short message. The page kept going in and out of focus and made the throbbing pick up in his head.

Next order of business, making it out the door. He stood up, swaying a little, found a bag, and put the note and his recently acquired gift inside. Next step, make it out the door.

Last step—going to Meg's. It wasn't easy, and it wasn't pretty, but somehow Sam drove his Corvette to her house. He set the bag on her step, fought his way through the return trip home, and made it to his couch.

Everything went black as soon as his head hit the pillow.

MEGAN WAS talking with the law firm's receptionist when her old classmate, Joey Driscoll, walked in. "How are you?" she called out. He had always been Mr. Cheerful in high school but wasn't smiling today.

"Have you been to the hospital to see Sam yet? They'll probably keep him overnight." She clasped the receptionist's desktop. Joe took her arm. "Hey, you okay?"

"What are you talking about? Has Sam been hurt? Is he sick? No one told me anything." Barely holding it together, she listened long enough to hear about the accident at work, grabbed her bag, and ran for the exit.

"SAMMY, ARE YOU all right? Sammy!" There was a loud pounding in Sam's head—no, it was at his front door. Sam slowly came out of a medicated fog and tried to identify the voice's owner.

Outside, there came a muffled cursing, the jiggling of a key in the lock, the slamming of the door. "Sammy, are you okay? Answer me!" *Megan's* voice, strained with fear.

Sam grimaced. Why had Michael told her? He called out hoarsely, "I'm in here, and could you please turn it down a notch?" His head was still protesting, and the thought of dealing with Megan's reluctant sympathy didn't help matters any.

The next thing he knew, Megan was at his side, gently touching his cheek and pressing a light kiss to his head. "Oh Sam, look at you! Joey Driscoll was in the law office at the end of the day and told me what happened. Why didn't you call me? You know I would've come."

Sam looked up at her with such quiet suffering that hurt Megan to see it. He would've liked nothing more than to have called her, had her with him at the hospital and curled up next to him here at his house. But it couldn't be that way, not now. "I didn't want to worry you. There's really nothing anyone can do. I just have to take it easy. I'll be fine."

Megan took a long, hard look at the man who had been her best friend, her tender and satisfying lover, her everything after they became adults . . . her life for the last twenty years. He was white as a ghost with eyes clouded by pain. There was an ugly knot on his head and deep red welts creeping down one arm, almost to his hand at this point. "Sam, please. This is me, Megan, you're talking to. You're *not* fine, and you *don't* know how to take it easy. I'm staying so I can take care of you."

Sam's good hand came up to cup her cheek, his eyes bright with unshed tears as he said the words that were killing him. "I'm sorry, Meg, but not now. After what's happened between us, I can't let you stay. It will hurt too much to know it's only for a little while, not for good; on that note, you might make the choice to come back to me out of sympathy. I'd always wonder if it was real. It means the world to me that you're here, that you care, but I really need to sleep more than anything, and I can't if you're here. Please, Meg. Try and understand."

Megan felt her own eyes begin to fill and didn't even wipe the tears away. "Sammy, I'm so sorry. Please don't make me leave."

"I have to. For both our sakes."

"I don't want to—it feels so wrong—but I will for you. Please call me if you need anything, anything at all, all right? Promise me. Swear to me."

"All right. I swear." He closed his eyes. It hurt too much to keep them open and watch her go again. He heard her crying as she shut the front door.

MEGAN CRIED THE entire way home, every instinct telling her to go back to Sam. However, she had to respect his wishes. Besides, she had made this mess, not him. *Stupid! Stupid! How could I have been so stupid to set up that meeting with a stranger through a dating service? Why hadn't I simply told Sam how I felt, gotten it all out of my system even if I hurt him and it took a lot of work to figure out a new path for us? That kind of pain would have been better than this.*

The decision to make a supremely dramatic point that Sam couldn't ignore, brush away, or talk her out of had begun one afternoon after a bad day at work. It was raining outside, and the same old routines were going on inside. She went home, dead on her feet, and Sam showed up with Chinese, *again*, because it was Tuesday, and the Chinese restaurant had a take-out deal on Tuesdays. She wanted to be alone, didn't want company.

Sam went home earlier than usual because she'd played up a bad headache. Megan had been poor company a lot lately, and she hated being that way around him. He was always so patient. She had been slouched on her recliner, depressed, when the E-LoveMe ad came on television and pulled her to the edge of her seat.

Megan always wondered about the internet dating services, toying with the idea of what match they'd find for her, but never dared admit, even to herself, that she needed to find out if Sam was the one-and-only man for her. *How could I ever explain my concerns without breaking his heart?*

He *never* had doubts about loving her; he was steadfast and sure of where he was headed and thought she was, too. Megan never told him about her fears . . .

but on that rainy Tuesday night, she listened to the questions circling in her mind and realized something for the first time: if she never took the risk, her love for Sam would always have a 'what if ' attached to it.

So she signed up, picked out a handsome photograph named Scott, agreed to meet him on that horrible Sunday, and now . . . she'd destroyed Sam's trust, apparently forever. The man who had been there for most of her life, for the good times and bad, needed her, but he wouldn't let her in.

Megan pulled in to her driveway and stopped dead when she saw the gift bag on her steps. Not even bothering to park in the garage, she stepped out and walked slowly to her porch. She sank down and picked up the bag. Reaching inside, eyes closed, her hand touched something with soft fur. It was an adorable teddy bear, its fur a rich chocolate, like Sam's eyes. She picked up his note, covering her mouth at the shaky handwriting scribbled on the page. Somehow, Sam had made it here, after he'd been hurt. Faithful—he was always unshakeable when it came to her.

> *Dear Meg,*
>
> *It's getting harder to sleep without you.*
> *I thought you might have the same*
> *trouble. Maybe this little guy will help,*
> *like Buddy, your childhood bear.*
>
> *Sam*

Buddy! Sam had given her the stuffed toy; they had been inseparable. Even in college, it sat on Meg's shelf until she donated it to a needy family who'd lost their home. Buddy had made it through the rough times, the lonely nights, all of the trials and tribulations of childhood.

He'd been a friend.

She buried her face in the fur of Buddy's replacement, openly sobbing now. She should go back to Sam, go back right now. She knew it in her heart, but she was too ashamed.

10

Day 8

A BURST OF thunder, certain to wake the dead, jerked Sam into a sitting position from a sound sleep and unleashed a colorful string of curses. His pain medication had worked well, putting him out for the night, but wore off abruptly with that unexpected movement. There was a strange quality to the light filtering in around his blinds; although it was after daybreak, it felt like twilight due to the dark clouds hovering in the sky.

Sam took his next dose of pain pills then gingerly stood up, doing his best to move his right arm as little as possible. He should've accepted the sling Brian offered. He took a trip to the bathroom where he briefly considered a shower but thought it was a lost cause; he couldn't get his shirt off by himself. He headed to the kitchen and stared at the coffee pot. He'd just decided it wasn't worth the effort involved when a heart-shaped rock resting on his counter caught his attention. The rain started pounding on the roof but couldn't drown out the images in his mind.

"Let's hunt for treasure, Sammy." Megan was nine, Sam was eleven, and they were on one of their many summer adventures in the woods behind their homes. They had made a list for a scavenger hunt. The young explorers forged into the forest, bringing bag lunches, pillow cases, a pencil, and their eagerness. They started at

the lunch hour; the sun was beginning its downward slope to the horizon when it was time to head home for dinner. Almost every item had been checked off, along with some additional prize finds to be showcased in Sam's tree house. Only one thing remained on the list—an extra special rock. They'd scoured for hours and argued back and forth over countless stones. None were good enough for Megan.

"Meggie, this is silly! Just pick a stupid rock!" Sam grumbled, kicking at the ground in aggravation. He was looking forward to his mom's barbecued chicken and that peanut butter and jelly sandwich was a really long time ago, like forever! He was over the moon for Meggie, but sometimes she drove him crazy!

Megan scrambled forward to catch the rock he'd unearthed with his slight temper tantrum and held it up in triumph. "Ta da! Look at this one! It's a heart—it's perfect!"

Sam shook his head—crazy girl—he didn't know why it was any better than all the rest, but he went along with it so they could get home to dinner. Megan skipped the entire way, her rock held high in the air while Sam had to jog to keep up. Her most valuable find sat on the patio table while they ate dinner; Meggie's face was smeared with barbecue sauce, and her smile was ready to split it in two. Silly girls!

Sam came back slowly from the memory, reluctant to leave the past. The rock had sat in his tree house for years, then on his nightstand in college, and finally in his own home. Maybe it was time for it to find another home. He pushed away from the counter and dug through a drawer for tissue paper. He fumbled with wrapping it with one hand, which wasn't the easiest, then did a repeat performance of yesterday's handwriting method. Hopefully, he'd be able to raise his right arm, and it would cooperate soon. Satisfied that it was the best he could manage, he settled on the couch. The challenge of getting the package to Megan would have to wait.

THE FAMILIAR sound of Michael's truck brought Sam out of a doze. A key jiggled in the lock; they each had keys for their houses. Michael walked in with a big smile. "I come bearing gifts—coffee and a bagel."

Sam smiled at the sight of the soggy bag and Michael's wet-dog appearance. "It's really coming down out there, eh? Thanks for making sure I won't starve. I know you won't believe this, but I can fend for myself."

Michael set the food down and sat down in the recliner in order to inhale his own coffee. He sighed in ecstasy. "I'm sure, but I had to make sure you received the most essential ingredient for your day, Gina's coffee. So, how's the patient this morning?" The bruising on Sam's temple and arm looked pretty mean, raising his best friend's concern.

"I won't lie. I've felt better, but it's not as bad as yesterday. I think I'll live." Sam took a long swallow of his coffee in order to reassure the mother hen. "Mmm . . . that'll do it. I appreciate your checking in on me."

Michael stood up to go. "Anytime. Call if you need anything." He turned and dubiously stared out the window. It was a good day to be a duck. "I wish I had a boat."

Sam shifted, making him wince as he jarred his shoulder. "Hey, Michael, could you do me a favor? There's a package on the counter. Would you drop it at Meg's? No questions. Please."

Michael nodded and scooped it up. "You've got it. Take it easy and don't worry about work. I've got it covered."

"Thanks buddy. Keep me posted."

The medication did its job, putting Sam to sleep for the next couple of hours. He roused briefly to eat his bagel and slipped off again. The next time he woke up, it was late afternoon. He took his next dose then rubbed at his face and eyes, trying to shake the grogginess that had taken over.

It was a losing battle due to the pills, but he tried to fight it with a shower. The couch made him sore and stiff; he was a slow, old man on the trip upstairs. He turned on the water and made it as hot as he could stand it. It was easy to slip out of his pajama bottoms. The true challenge was the shirt. His right shoulder would not cooperate as he tried to raise it. In the end, he tugged at the sleeve with his left arm and twisted and turned, crying out with the stabs of pain. He finally managed to get it over his head and stepped into the shower. The steady, hot stream provided a much-needed massage when a voice drifted his way.

"Sammy, it's Meg. I was on my way home, and I had to check on you. I couldn't help it. Are you okay?" She hovered anxiously outside the bathroom door.

Sam pressed his forehead to the wall then pulled back as his head protested. "Yeah, I'll be right out." He soaped and rinsed to the best of his ability then stepped out. He wrapped himself in a towel with one hand, frustrated by the awkwardness. He spoke through the closed door. "You didn't have to do this."

"Yes, I did. How can I help you?"

Sam bit off a curse as he managed his pajama pants but knew he'd never win the fight with the shirt, not without making any noise. He closed his eyes in surrender. "I can't lift my arm. Can you please help me with my t-shirt?"

Megan opened the door carefully and stepped inside, trying to hide her alarm at the sight of the ugly bruising on Sam's temple and arm. She picked up his shirt and very gently slipped it up his arms and over his head. Her eyes softened as she saw the pain written on his face when he had to shift his shoulder. "Is there anything else I can do?"

He closed his eyes in order to shield his emotions. Why couldn't they go back to the way things were? It would be so easy to fall back together, right now, but he would never know if it was real or not. "Just give me a few minutes of privacy, please."

By the time Sam collected himself to make the journey downstairs, Megan had hot soup and a sandwich waiting for him on the coffee table. He eased himself down with a forced smile. "You really didn't have to do this, Meg. I'm not helpless." Except when it came to her. He was made helpless at the site of her, blonde curls springing up from the rain, impossibly sexy in her business suit. It took all he had not to pull her onto the couch and beg her to stay.

She sat down in the chair closest to him and fiddled with a bracelet, unwilling to meet his gaze. "I know, but you deserve a little TLC. You always do it for everyone else. It's your turn."

It was killing him being this close to her, yet Sam forced his tone to be light. "Well, have some dinner with me."

Megan became flustered. "I only made enough for you." *Why hadn't I thought about how awkward this would be? Sure, just feed him and leave. Nice going, Meg.*

Sam solved the problem, as he so often did, by handing her half a sandwich. "Here, we can share. The medication is killing my appetite. I couldn't eat it all, anyway."

Megan blushed as she accepted, feeling the brush of his hand against hers. "Thank you." She unobtrusively watched as Sam took much longer to eat, as if it was a chore.

The soup was more of a dilemma. Sam balanced the

bowl on his lap and managed to lift his right arm the small distance needed to steady the bowl. He considered it a small victory even though it had him in a cold sweat. His left hand trembled slightly but otherwise didn't give him away. "Thanks. That was good, but I'm getting tired. This medicine is kicking my butt."

Megan knew it was more than just the medicine. She stood up and kissed the top of his unruly brown hair. "All right, I'll let you get some rest." She picked up the dishes and took them to the kitchen. She cleaned up and peeked out into the living room. Sam's lashes were dark on his pale skin. He was already dozing on the couch. She let herself out.

One more stop before going home. She'd been to the florist that afternoon, and a large pot of flowers sat on the floor of the passenger seat. Time to get it to the right place, talk to someone that would always listen, could solve a problem, no matter how big or how small. The rain, steady throughout the day, slowed and came to a stop.

The cemetery was quiet; everyone else was home with their families, sitting down at the dinner table, recounting their day. The sun peeked through the clouds, touched down on the horizon, leaving a wash of pinks and purples in the sky. Megan sank down by James O'Malley's stone and set the flowers beside it. "Hi Dad. I brought your daisies. I know how they made you smile. You always used to say, 'There's my Daisy,' when I'd come by." She called Sam's father 'Dad' as naturally as she'd called her own by that title.

The pain, buried deep within, surfaced, choking her and bringing tears with it. "I . . . I've come for Sammy's sake. He's hurt and needs someone to watch over him. I figure you have some pull up there. Maybe you and God could stop by." She lifted her hand to the stone, traced its letters, let her fingertips rest on the cool surface.

No peace today. Sam said that he felt better whenever he came here. Megan felt otherwise; it was a torment, the reminder of what had been lost. *Stop lying to yourself.* It was more than that. Her guilt wouldn't let peace in; she didn't deserve it when Sam was in trouble and she was the cause.

Darkness fell, and still she knelt on the cold ground, her clothes becoming damp. It didn't matter. A breeze picked up around her, brushed her cheek, settled her. Megan brushed at her cheeks and gave a little nod. "Thanks, Dad. I know you'll take care of him. I'll do my best, too, but first I've got to straighten myself out." She stood and walked to her car. The skies opened again as if waiting until her visit was over.

The rain continued to pour on the short drive to her house; she could hardly see the road and was relieved when her house came in sight. It was a shorter distance to park by her door rather than in the garage. She ran up the steps to find a package tucked in her mailbox. This time she read the note first in the dim light of her kitchen, feeling the weight of the tissue-wrapped bundle in her hand, a weight that was not nearly as heavy as the one on her heart.

> *Dear Meg,*
>
> *Remember the search for this perfect rock? We had to look all day until I found it for you by accident. Finding you was no accident.*
>
> *Sam*
>
> *P.S. This rock is to remind you that you have my heart forever.*

The tears, like a well that never dried, were back; in her search for the road to happiness, she'd taken a wrong turn and brought Sam with her. Megan went to her room, stripped out of her wet clothes, and stepped into the shower. The hot water ran over her body, but it was not enough to take away the inner chill. She was not wrong for wanting more from life than the quiet world of Cordial Creek and a boring but secure job as a paralegal. But that didn't mean she had to give up Sam.

She pulled on old, flannel pajamas and climbed into bed, turned out the lights, and stared at the ceiling. It was too early for bed. Her stomach was empty but not as empty as her heart. *Sammy, I'm so sorry. I need to take charge of who I am and what I want if I'm going to win you back on terms we can both love.*

11

Day 9

FUNNY THING . . . bodies could mend more easily than hearts; Sam's aches and pains were already improving. It was day three of his captivity, and he thought he would go nuts with boredom; he felt well enough to think he could do more than lay around the house until he tried and found out otherwise.

The day began with sunshine and a nip to the air that only made it harder to be indoors. The need to do something, anything, even made him feel claustrophobic. It pushed him to dress and sit outside on his front step, foot tapping with his restlessness.

Michael pulled in, like clockwork, to check in on him. The moment he stepped out of his truck, Sam was on his feet. "I'm coming with you. I'll sit in the office and stay at my desk."

Michael raised his hands in the air, revealing a coffee in one hand and a bag for Sam in the other. "Whoa! I'm just the delivery boy, making sure you survive and that you are following doctor's orders. That means *no way*. Liability issues. Corporate policy. Hey, guess who made the rules? You did."

Sam grabbed the bag. "Thanks for stopping by. Don't get too used to this, because I will be back on Monday."

"Hang in there. This is probably good for you, since

you work too hard. I'll catch ya later."

Sam doubted this could be good for anyone. He banged around the house after Michael left but didn't accomplish anything. There were a thousand channels on his TV—what a waste!—but nothing worth watching. He'd cut back on his pain medication to avoid being so sleepy; now he was sore and antsy. Megan did not stop to see him, and he worried about that. Overall, he was in a miserable mood. He was staring out the window, contemplating a walk down to the lake, when the sound of a car announced someone's arrival.

A bright, orange Volkswagen—it matched its owner's sunny personality—was parked outside his door. The owner, Mabel Thompson, approached his steps with a box and bouquet of sunflowers. He couldn't help smiling and was surprised she hadn't come sooner; she was the town busybody but had a heart of gold, like the locket she always wore. Her gray hair was wound in a braid on top of her head, her glasses perched on her nose, and she wore a handmade sweater and flowered dress, much like she'd worn for Sam's entire life. Her quick, firm stride did not match her age, and she gave his door a hearty knock.

Sam pulled the door open just as she was about to put his package down on the steps. "Good afternoon, Miss Mabel. What brings you here on this fine day? Things too slow for you in town?"

Mabel's eyes held a mischievous glint as she reached out and gave Sam a pat on his arm. "You know I've come to see you with my own eyes, my boy. I couldn't stand another minute. The boys from work have been stopping in daily, each one telling me about your catastrophe, until I thought you were close to dying."

He laughed and looped an arm around her shoulders. "Well, Miss Mabel, it seems reports of my imminent death have been highly exaggerated. I'm fine, just a little sore. Would you like to come in and have some lunch with me?"

She flapped a hand as if shooing away a fly. "Oh, heavens, no, child. I've got to get back to the post office. I've never opened late from my lunch break, not once in fifty years, and I'm not about to start today. I can see for myself that you'll do, though I think you might be more than a little sore. I've brought you some of my chocolate jumbles. I know they're your favorite. You go rest up, Sammy, and stop in to see me when you're right as rain."

Sam took the gifts and gave her a light kiss on the cheek in return. "Thank you, Miss Mabel. You were just what I needed today. How on earth did you manage sunflowers this late in autumn, anyway?"

Mabel shrugged, cheeks flushed with color from the kiss. "An old woman has to keep some secrets. I'll tell you one of them though. If I was forty years younger, I'd be after you, young fella. Now skedaddle and take care of yourself." She had even more of a spring in her step on her way back to her car, followed by Sam's laughter.

MABEL'S VISIT, lunch, and a few cookies gave Sam some badly needed motivation. He put together Meg's gift for the day and made the decision to walk to her place. The leaves were in full color, the air continued to feel crisp, and the sun was bright overhead. He slipped on his coat and considered that simple act an achievement. He took it slow and enjoyed himself. Meg's front door step provided a perfect place to rest and gather energy for the return trip. He didn't linger to avoid being noticed by her neighbors.

The fresh air and view helped improve Sam's mood, but his shoulder was protesting by the time he dragged up his own steps. A full dose of medication and an extra-long, hot shower were in order, followed by a heating pad when he climbed in to bed. Sleep easily found him and carried him into the evening.

MEGAN SIGHED AS she pulled into her driveway. She was so lost in thought that she didn't even notice any of the scenery on her way home. Sam's house had tugged hard enough on her heart that she actually pulled over. She sat with her head on the steering wheel, heart pounding, and waited for at least fifteen minutes. However, she didn't give in and continued on home just as the sun sank over the horizon.

He had asked for twenty days of separation; although it had not been said quite that way. Twenty days to let the dust settle; twenty days to let Sam find ways to remind her of all the reasons she had once loved him.

I still love you, she wanted to tell him. *It's never been about not loving you.*

Sitting in the car didn't provide Megan with any magical answers. Her feet dragged on the path to her front steps. Sam had visited, once again, to hang a gift bag on her door. There were footprints leading to it and away. It had rained recently, and the ground was muddy. Megan glanced in her driveway for tire tracks, but there were none. Eyebrows raised in disbelief, she followed the footsteps until they disappeared into the forest. That stubborn man had walked here!

Megan walked inside, shaking her head. She didn't look inside her package until she was on the sofa with her regular cup of tea.

Sam had sent her the DVD of *An Officer and a Gentleman*.

Dear Meg,

You've been feeling down for a long time and have hidden it from me. It bothers me to think that you've been unhappy and I never knew.

Here's one of your favorite movies. I can't even count how many movies we've watched together or how many times we've watched this one. I especially like this one because Richard Gere wins the girl.

Sam

12

Day 10

SATURDAYS MEANT sleeping in; they were actually reserved for such luxury. Traditions must be kept, in Sam's mind, allowing him to give in to the needs of his body and mind. But not this much "in."

His eyes didn't even open until noon—unheard of on a normal weekend. He never slept this late even in college. He also felt uncharacteristically lazy. If ever he'd needed an argument against drugs, the way he felt after several days on pain medication gave him plenty of ammunition.

A shower was the first step in his revitalization. Lunch also provided a big kick in the pants, seeing as there wasn't any food in the house. Cupboards did not magically refill themselves. The groceries were not going to come to him, and he refused to ask anyone else to shop for him. He tossed some laundry in the washer, took care of the few dishes in the sink, and walked out to his garage. Michael had brought his truck home with one of the guys from work; that left Sam a choice between the Vette and his pickup. The truck won due to practicality.

Sam climbed up into the cab, ready to go, when the sight of the stick shift gave him pause. He had been using his right arm a bit more. However, he wasn't sure he had the strength and mobility for this drive. There was only one way to find out—just do it.

An O'Malley never turned away from a challenge. He stuck the key in the ignition and shifted into reverse. Some colorful cursing followed with the sensation of wrenching a muscle in his shoulder. It did not improve for the duration of the trip into town. It only felt worse upon arrival at the supermarket.

Sam parked, chewing his tongue as pain shot up his arm. This had been a *great* idea. Why feel better? These days, feeling lousy was a way of life.

A tapping on the window broke his concentration. Michael opened the door then crossed his arms in indignation. "Do you mind telling me what the hell you're doing? I bet you could be arrested for driving a stick with that barely functioning arm."

"I needed food, all right?" This was a test. Learning to get by on his own, without Meg by his side.

Michael gestured toward the store. "I guess you've come to the right place. Let's get on with it."

When they finished shopping, Michael loaded everything into the truck then handed his keys to Sam. "You take my automatic, and I'll drive this bucket of yours home." He took off before there was time for any argument.

My life has gone to hell in a handbasket, Sam thought.

AMAZINGLY, HE managed to climb into the fishing boat without pitching overboard. The water was warm, the air comfortable, and the fish nibbled from time to time. Michael kept trying to bring up Megan, and Sam kept ignoring him.

It seemed early when the sun began to slide down in the sky. Sam felt himself starting to stiffen up and ache. The medicine could only last so long, and the day out in the boat wasn't the best therapy for Sam's body even if it was perfect for his spirit. "I don't know about you, but I'm getting hungry. Why don't we head back?"

Michael straightened up with a big grin. "You bet. You're milking this bum shoulder, aren't you? Getting out of work, avoiding grocery bags, shirking on the rowing—" He dodged a beer can that came flying his way.

Sam sat up straight and tall no matter how much it hurt. His expression matched the way his body felt. "I don't like it one bit, Michael. I feel like a slacker."

His friend adjusted his own mood to mirror Sam's. "Buddy, cut it out. You always work harder and longer than anyone else. Don't you dare feel bad when you need a break."

They drove back to Sam's place in silence. Michael poked his head in the fridge upon arrival and shook his head. "No, not gonna do. Need pizza. Be right back."

After he drove off, Sam shook his head and sat down in the recliner. He felt like he'd forgotten something . . . *Megan*. He hurried to the kitchen and paced back and forth. A rundown of the day provided inspiration. He jotted a quick note, grabbed her gift, and headed out to the truck. A sense of urgency made him rush. She couldn't think he had forgotten, and Michael didn't need to know where he was going.

Sam climbed in and threw the gear into reverse, cursing at the renewed stab of pain in his arm. He peeled out and managed to shift into second for the brief trip. Her car wasn't in the driveway. He left her present on the porch and drove back home in record time. The couch called to him as he walked in, gripping his right arm and covered in a cold sweat. He'd just closed his eyes when Michael returned.

I almost forgot about her.

And clearly she's forgotten about me.

MEGAN HAD spent the day with Sophie Farrielo, her best friend from high school. They made a point of getting together a couple times a month. Jobs and a love life didn't have to mean giving up on each other. Shopping, lunch, and a movie often brightened Megan's moods.

Not this time. Megan had almost cancelled. She couldn't bring herself to talk about Sam or what she had done to their relationship. As for his efforts to save it, she wanted that kept private. She was guarding something precious and rare, experienced by few. He'd put his heart on the line. A very real headache forced her to beg off dinner and seek refuge at home.

It was dark when Megan climbed her steps to discover a four-pack of strawberry daiquiri wine coolers tucked against the door. "Oh, Sam," she said hoarsely. She walked inside, opened a bottle, and read the attached note.

> *Dear Meg,*
>
> *Usually, after a rough day, we'd sit together down by the lake on a warm day and dangle our feet in the water. If it was cold, we'd curl up in front of the fire. You'd lean into me, and I'd lean into you. We'd share a bottle, maybe two, and everything else would go away. There was just you and me. I hope it does the trick for you tonight.*
>
> *Sam*

13

Day 11

EVERY SUNDAY morning brought hope for a new week ahead. Sunlight slipped through the cracks in the blinds and pricked at Sam's eyelids. Cool air crept in through a slightly opened window and finished the job of waking him up. He rubbed at his face and opened the blind; the day looked promising. The hot water in the shower made him feel glad to be awake, because his shoulder only protested a little. Perhaps the exertion from the day before had actually helped to loosen it up. He felt better, and that was all that mattered.

A sense of calm settled over Sam along with his cup of coffee out on the back deck. He knew how he needed to start this day—church was calling. He didn't go every week, but he tried to go often. It was God's day, a day when everything seemed possible and past mistakes could be forgotten. Church was the place where the lost always found their way.

It seemed only natural that Meg's gift for the day would have a connection with Sunday. It took a bit of searching through drawers and boxes, but Sam finally found what he was looking for. He managed to place it on Meg's doorknob bright and early; she hadn't even woken up yet if the newspaper on her step was any indication. Then he made his way to church.

The little, white building was quickly filling with

friends and neighbors. It felt good to be welcomed with smiles, greetings, and familiar faces. They were an extended family to all who gathered. Sam's mother, Mare O'Malley, lit up when her son brushed her cheek with a kiss and wrapped an arm around her. "Morning, Mom. How's the most beautiful woman in the world today?"

Mare blushed from her son's compliment and slid over to make room on the pew. "Samuel, you're always so sweet to me."

His coffee eyes were warm as he spoke softly to one of the most important people in his life. "You taught me how to be that way."

He knew that looking at him brought both pleasure and pain to his mother. The resemblance to his father as a young man was so pronounced that she said she sometimes felt as if she'd stepped back in time. She often teased Sam that the only thing he'd gotten from her was his stubborn nature. Sam loved how she compared him to his dad—kind, fair, honest, faithful, hard-working—*Both of you good men*, she said, *through and through.*

But I lack something Dad had, Sam thought. *He had a talent for making Mom happy. He sensed when she was unhappy. Not like me. I overlooked all the signs that Megan was miserable.*

Mare's eyes filled with concern, her fingers flitting over the bruise on his temple. "What's this?"

Sam took her hand and squeezed it. "There was a minor accident at work. It's nothing."

His mother could see her way to the truth in any matter concerning her son. She knew he was sugarcoating the injury but let it go for the moment. Her next question was harder to brush aside. "Where's Meg?"

"She's sleeping in today." The service began,

delaying any further conversation. An hour later, the congregation gathered for coffee and refreshments in the refectory. The room hummed with chitchat and camaraderie. Several of Sam's coworkers stopped to greet and check in on their boss, causing Mare to raise her eyebrows questioningly at her son. She listened intently to each exchange; nothing made it past her.

Pastor Tony D'Angelo approached Sam and his mother, bringing a big smile for two of his favorites from his congregation. Italian to the core from his black hair to skin the shade of a golden tan, he did everything in a big way. Today was no exception. He gave Sam a hearty slap on the back, jarring Sam's shoulder and making him wince. Pastor Tony let go immediately. "Sam, what's wrong? Whatever I did, I'm sorry."

Sam shook his head. His mother answered for him. "I assume it's from the *minor* accident at work that my son failed to tell me about." She glared in disapproval.

"It's much better now, really," Sam said quickly. "How are you, Pastor?"

When it was time to leave, Mare linked her arm in Sam's as they walked out. "I insist you come to Sunday dinner and allow me to mother you, since you *didn't* give me that chance earlier this week."

"I didn't want you to worry. All right, I'll follow you home to dinner."

MEGAN'S MORNING began like a typical Sunday with tea and comics, yet she couldn't find pleasure in these comforts. Sunday was one day she definitely did not like to spend alone. She glanced at the clock and sighed. It was too late for church, and it would have been awkward if Sam was there. She missed heading over to his mother's for Sunday dinner, but that was out of the question.

What I wouldn't give for a Sunday drive with Sam.

She sat at the kitchen table, listless and unwilling to do anything. Sam's gift, a small box which he'd tucked inside her newspaper, sat unopened on the table. Finally she lifted the lid to find a tiny cross of gold on a slender chain. Leave it to Sam to bring church to her. She slipped it over her head, resting her hand on it, and devoted her attention to the note.

> *Dear Meg,*
>
> *I've needed a little faith lately—okay, maybe a lot as I try to understand that everything I thought was true between you and me might not be. I send this to you to remind you to have faith as well. You can always have faith in me. I also wanted to thank you for being here all these years, but especially on the day I received this cross. It was the day we buried Dad, a day when my faith was badly shaken. You pulled me through it. It's time for you to have this now when your faith is shaky. I hope it will help you the way that you've always helped me.*
>
> *Sam*

Megan touched the cross; it brought it all back, scars that would never be completely healed and still burned painfully when rubbed again.

Mr. O'Malley's death, just two years ago, had been hard on her—he'd become like a father. Sam was devastated and withdrew a little inside himself; maybe that was the moment something changed between them.

He was strung tight, a bow ready to snap, struggling to pick up the pieces for his mother, raw from his efforts to keep himself from falling apart.

That night, Megan had slept in the tree house in the O'Malley backyard. It felt right to go there, close to the man who had been part of raising her. Crawling inside in jeans and a t-shirt, she stretched out on their old sleeping bag from childhood and listened to rain pounding on the ceiling. The skies had opened up the moment the funeral home took Mr. O'Malley's body away, and hadn't stopped since. Fitting that the whole world should be crying.

Sleep wouldn't come. She spent the night staring up at the ceiling, her heart breaking, crying harder than she'd ever cried in her life until it was hard to breathe and she thought she'd never stop. A gradual lightening of the sky from black to gray came with the dawn and found Megan kneeling at the window, head bowed; she prayed, but she wasn't sure why. For Mr. O'Malley? For his wife? Or for Sam and herself, to find a way through the pain? So suddenly an important father figure had been torn from their lives, and it left a wound that ran deep.

There was a creaking on the ladder. Megan wiped at her cheeks and caught her reflection in the mirror they'd hung to play "Mirror, Mirror on the Wall," another adventure from childhood. She was a fright, hair a mess, eyes puffy and red. Any attempt at making herself presentable was hopeless. The sight of Mrs. O'Malley, climbing inside, took Megan off guard, brought her to the verge of tears again. "Mrs. O, what are you doing up here?"

Mrs. O'Malley was wet from walking through the rain; however, the marks on her face were from her tears, close to the surface now and for a long time to come. "I thought I heard something up here and had a hunch it was you. What are you doing up here all alone, Meggie? Come here, my girl." She opened her arms wide.

With a sob catching in her throat, Megan stepped into the older woman's arms and felt her trembling. "I'm so sorry, Mrs. O. You have enough to worry about without worrying about me. It's just . . . Sam is the one person I could talk to at a time like this, and he's got too much on his shoulders to carry me, too. Mr. O built this place; he used to sit up here with us from time to time, join in our games. I feel like he's here. Is that silly?"

"No, honey, not at all. Jim's everywhere around this place. I'm not sure if that's a comfort or a curse right now. As for being able to talk this through, I know how you feel. Jim was my shoulder to lean on, my best friend; he knew me better than I knew myself. I miss him. I want to hold his hand, look at him, have him help me through this. But he can't, and I won't put that kind of burden on Sam! It will hurt too much!" Mare O'Malley was a strong woman, but her husband's death made her fragile; it seemed like she could break at a touch.

Megan held on tight as Mrs. O'Malley broke down in her arms and began to stroke her graying hair, like she was a child. "You can talk to me, Mrs. O, any time. If you don't feel like talking, you can lean on me. My shoulders are pretty strong, too. We'll get through this, somehow, together." They sat there on the ratty old sleeping bag and listened to the rain fall. When they could pick their hearts up again, they helped each other down.

Three days later, at the funeral, it was Meg's turn to be strong for Sam, coming to him, hoping it would give him strength. She prayed for strength now as she closed her fingers tightly around his cross, that God would lead her and Sam in the right direction.

Sam stood in his childhood bedroom, staring with unseeing eyes into the backyard, memory upon memory of his father replaying through his mind. He had spent the night at the house to keep his mother company; she had just left for the hairdresser and then he would take her to the funeral home. His shirt was unbuttoned, his tie still on the bed, a tiny cross clutched in his hand.

Megan slipped behind him and wrapped her arms around his waist. "How are you doing?"

A tremor ran through his body as his voice came out rough with emotion. "I'm twenty eight years-old, and I have to bury my father today. I thought this wouldn't happen for at least another thirty or forty years." He choked up. "I thought this would never happen." He was raw with the pain, shaken to the core, finding it hard to stay on his feet.

Megan stepped in front of him and looped her arms around his neck, tears sliding down her cheeks. "I know. He was my other dad. I can't believe he's gone."

Sam bent his head and buried it in her shoulder. She could feel him shaking as he finally, silently broke. He'd been so strong—strong enough to catch his father the moment a heart attack took him down while they were repairing the back porch; strong enough to begin CPR, shouting to Megan to call nine-one-one, calling to his father to hold on, that he loved him, in case those were the last words his father would hear. He was a rock for his mother when the doctor broke the news that Jim O'Malley was gone.

In the quiet of his father's house, with the comfort of Megan's touch and the knowledge that his mother would not hear him, he crumbled. It was up to Megan to help pick up the pieces, but first she let him fall apart. It was something they all had to do in order to heal. She held him until the shaking stopped and he pulled away. Tears ran down his face for the first time since it all happened. His eyes, usually so clear and so calm, were tortured. "What am I going to do without him?"

Megan shook her head. "Nobody knows yet, but we'll find out together." She took his hand in hers and felt something hard wrapped around his fingers. "What's this?" she asked, glancing down.

Sam cleared his throat and wiped at his face. "My mother gave it to me this morning. It was Dad's baptismal cross. She thought I should have it to keep him close all of the time."

Megan took it from his hand and slipped the chain over his head. She pressed her finger to the delicate cross. "This is a treasure, but you don't need this to have your dad stay with you. He'll always be here." She pressed a kiss to his chest. "In your heart. Where he will never die as long as you remember him."

Sam gathered her close in an embrace that was strong enough to crush her. "I've always heard that saying, 'You're the man of the family now, boy.' I'm almost thirty years old, and I'm like a boy without a father. But I'm the man of this family, now. It's time to get more serious about my responsibilities. What I owe my mother and this town and you. Put down roots."

As if he weren't so firmly rooted in Cordial Creek, such a devoted son and loving boyfriend and responsible businessman, already. It was the day he decided that there would never be any other path for him. That Meg would have to accept that.

MEGAN SLIPPED back to the present as she placed the cross on her own neck. She kissed it and softly whispered, "We'll never forget you, Dad. I haven't forgotten Sammy either. I just need some time."

SAM STOOD on the back porch, leaning against the post, as he gazed out at the pond in his mother's backyard. He squeezed his eyes shut as images of his father's last minutes on this earth, their last moments together, played through his mind. He didn't pull them up on purpose; they were unavoidable. He willed his thoughts away from that scene two years ago and made a conscious effort to think about the many good memories instead.

So many of those memories included Megan and her family. However, Megan was not here today—and her parents had moved to Florida a few years ago.

His mother came out and took his arm. "Come in, honey. Dessert is ready." She looked up at him with understanding; she had permanent images of that day as well, of her strong, vibrant husband turned to an empty shell in the arms of their son. Sam had been so strong and fought so hard—first to save his father, then with his grief. He was too strong, holding up everyone else at the time and attempting to be her shield. He still acted as a shield, trying to protect Mare from pain and worry.

They avoided the dining room table and the painful reminder of a father's chair. The small, cozy setting of the kitchen table was the best choice. Sam sighed in contentment as he took a bite of chocolate cream pie. "So good, Mom. No one cooks like you."

Mare basked in his compliments. "Thank you, sweetheart, although Megan is doing quite well in the kitchen, too." She paused then reached out to touch his hand. "What's going on with Meg? I can't think of the last time she missed a Sunday dinner."

Sam stared down at his pie, unable to look his mother in the eye. "We're going through a bit of a rough patch. It's nothing major, Mom. I'll let you know if anything big happens."

Mare gave his hand a gentle squeeze. "I'm always here, Sam, with an ear to listen and a shoulder to lean on. Mothers are good at that. You don't have to handle everything alone."

He kissed her hand and met her eyes this time, letting the love shine through. "I know, Mom. I'll take you up on your offer if I need to. I promise."

Day 12

MICHAEL ARRIVED early at work; since he'd been in charge, he'd actually managed to come in at Sam's normal time. Michael stepped up next to him and started swinging a hammer in time with Sam's. Eventually, Sam stopped to take a break, giving Michael a chance to call out, "Thanks for taking over the job of being in early; it's for the birds. I'm going back to being habitually later than you, all right?"

Sam laughed, his good mood restored by being back at work. "No problem. I can even make it in earlier if you'd like."

The rest of the crew wandered in within the next half hour, and it was business as usual. The project was on schedule, nearly done, and then it would be time to begin another. Sam worked with the crews in the morning then switched to the office in the afternoon when his shoulder needed a rest. At the end of the day, he stopped by the diner for a quick bite. Gina recommended the hot turkey sandwich.

He dropped off Megan's present and went home. It still took getting used to, an empty house, no one at the table, no one picking up the phone. Made him realize how tough it had to be for Mom. There was no prospect of Dad coming back. At least Sam had hope.

The computer and a book were his companions for the evening after a long, hot shower. It passed the time; everything did, but nothing really filled the void; all were poor substitutes for Meg's warmth and light. There were eight days left, eight days to find out if his forever would be with or without her.

14

MEGAN CAME home at the end of another day of sifting through piles of legal documents either literally or via computers, her eyes tired and shoulders aching. She took a shower then wandered aimlessly around her house. This separation taught her the value of being with someone; being alone was definitely not her goal, nor did she want to be with anyone but Sam. So confused. How had she become so confused?

She sat down on her bed. Night fell. In her hands was Sam's latest gift. She'd waited until then, giving herself something to look forward to. There was a journal with a beautiful photograph of a rose on the cover. His note was written inside, a permanent reminder every time she would open it.

> *Dear Meg,*
>
> *I don't think the clock has ever ticked this slowly in my life, and yet I'm scared to death that time is moving too fast, because I don't know how this will all end. I remember when we were kids—you were always scribbling stories or writing in a diary. I found your secret hiding place every time, picked the lock, and read your stories. You were so mad at me! I didn't know why. We told each other everything.*

*There were no secrets. Strange, that there
are secrets now. There must be . . .
because I didn't know this was coming,
couldn't see it.*

Sam

Day 13

Sam grew bolder on day thirteen, deciding it would
be a good luck number rather than a bad one. What was
that saying? Desperate times called for desperate
measures. Megan woke early that morning to find a box
and note sitting on her kitchen table.

Dear Meg,

*You've always been my lady luck and
always will be. These will help you to
carry some extra luck with you whenever
you need it, too.*

Sam

P.S. Don't worry. They're cheap.

The box held tiny, delicate ladybug earrings. They
were red with black spots and looked like they could take
off and fly at a moment's notice. Megan put them on
immediately.

Don't worry. They're cheap.

She smiled through tears at the inside joke. It took
her back twelve years ago to another fall day when Sam
was leaving for college. She'd hated those college years,
first when he was away and then for the two years after
he graduated when it was her turn to go.

While everyone else looked forward to the
adventure and kicking off the dust of high school and

hometowns, Megan had dreaded it. College, to her, was like a prison sentence, something to be endured, not a pleasure. Ironic, now that she thought she wanted to escape Cordial Creek for good.

The air was cool, and the leaves were just beginning to change. Where had the summer gone, and how had this day arrived already? Megan still had two more years of high school. Anything could happen in two years, especially here at Sam's college. He'd be far away from her and Cordial Creek, making new friends and meeting countless, beautiful girls. Megan had already seen plenty to make her feel insecure. It happened all the time; as soon as someone went away to college, everyone at home was forgotten. How could she compete with the excitement and the variety? How could she hold him when they were so far apart? To expect him to wait, to leave others alone, to be a saint . . . too much. She asked too much.

Megan sat on the bed in his dorm, fighting back tears. Jim and Mare had gone outside to give them a private moment. Sam had just opened the care package she'd given him—his favorite snacks, a warm blanket, slipper socks, stationary for writing home, and a picture of him and her from his senior prom.

Sam sat down next to her and pulled her close, struggling to contain his own emotions. "Meg, I love the picture. It will sit on my nightstand so I go to sleep and wake up to you every day. Thank you for everything. I have something for you, too."

He handed Megan a tiny box. She opened it to find a delicate, heart-shaped pendant of gold with a diamond teardrop in the middle. "Sam, it's beautiful, but what if I lose it?"

Sam laughed. "Don't worry, it's cheap. I still remember how upset you were about that expensive necklace I gave you. The one that you lost when the chain broke."

She burst out laughing in return. "'It's cheap.' The way you said that. 'It's cheap.'"

"Well, it is. I'm honest." He touched the pendant. "This is to remind you how much I love you and how much it hurts to be away, even for a day. I want you to wear it every day as a symbol—not

having to worry about losing it. I promise I will always come back to you. There's no one else that can hold a candle to my girl." He pulled her close and kissed her, not caring when his tears started to mingle with hers.

Megan reached up and held his face in her hands. "I won't ever take it off." She kissed him once more then ran out to join his family before she completely broke down. She would never know how Sam cried that night after she walked out.

Megan reached inside her shirt now and pulled out the heart necklace, tarnished and old. She had kept her promise; she'd never taken it off. She cried harder as she thought about Sam's promise to her. He had kept it with absolute faith. She was the one who'd wavered.

Day 14

THE NEXT DAY, a gift bag waited on her desk at work when she returned from running an errand. What—did he have spies? When had he managed to slip in here? No one seemed to know; perhaps the lawyers were in on it, making their own efforts at a love connection. Megan opened the present to find an iPod already loaded with music and of course, Sam's note.

> *Dear Meg,*
>   *If we have a soundtrack for our years together, it's Keith Urban's songs.*
>
>   *Sam*

SHE SPENT HER lunch break walking through their small town, the music plugged in to her ears, her mind tuned to the past. Sam had the power to bring it all back, make it feel fresh and real again.

Megan had finally made it through college. She thought graduation day would never come, that she wouldn't survive the wait, but all that hard work paid off. The ceremony was over, her car was packed to the brim, and Sam was driving her home. He had come up with her family and remained after they began the return trip.

He sat behind the wheel. The radio was cranked up, playing Keith Urban's "Who Wouldn't Wanna Be Me," and Megan had her window wide open. "Yes! I am out of here, and I'm never coming back!" she shouted out the window as the university receded in her side mirror. "Hello future! Here I come!"

Sam reached across and took her hand, high spirits bubbling over at the prospect of seeing her every day again. "I can't believe it's over and I've got you back. Between my years in college and yours, that's six years of our lives that we had to spend time apart. I don't plan on doing that ever again."

Megan slid across the seat and leaned her head on his shoulder. "Me, neither. It feels so good to be going home to stay. We need to do something special to celebrate before I settle down to real life."

Sam hung an arm over her shoulders, a grin stretching from ear to ear. "Let's elope! Just kidding—I've already got something in mind."

He looked like the Cheshire Cat or a cat that had just swallowed a really big mouse. "What do you have up your sleeve, O'Malley?" Megan could still feel her heart pounding at the thought of marriage. The crazy thing was, a part of her wanted to do it. Be crazy, stupid, or both and not care! After all, it was Sam. Sam could make anything work.

"You'll just have to wait and see." Sam refused to give in, no matter how much she begged for a clue. He turned the music up louder and allowed the CD, Golden Road, *to play through its entirety. Megan wasn't sure whether she should be in a huff or amused but decided to go with it. They weren't heading toward home; rather, the signs pointed to Saratoga, New York.*

They joined the flow of traffic entering the Saratoga

Performing Arts Center. Megan had never been there, but she'd heard that it was a wonderful, open-air theater. She looked up at Sam, who had become Mr. Mischief when he opened her door. "Sammy, who are we going to see?"

A shake of the head and, "Wait a few more seconds," was his only answer. They walked on a bridge that spanned high above a manmade creek, surrounded by trees until it felt like they were being tucked in to the forest. An attendant collected their ticket stubs, and then it was on to the theater, open except for a roof with brown colors that blended with the landscape. It was crowded, seats almost filled, but Sam brought Megan down to the front row. She still had no clue who the performer was until the lights went down and Keith Urban walked out on stage. He was her favorite performer, and one that Sam enjoyed as well. Megan turned to Sam, bubbling with excitement. "I can't believe you did this, Sammy! Thank you!"

It was one of the best concerts ever. They waited by the tour bus after the show and even managed an autograph. The night wasn't over; Sam had booked reservations at the Gideon Putnam, an elegant, renowned hotel in the Saratoga area and favorite of wealthy horse racing fans. They stayed up half the night, talking about the concert and all the songs they loved from the Golden Road tour. It made them think of the golden future before them. After two nights in Saratoga, they headed home. Megan hummed "Tangled Up in Love," an older song of Keith's from The Ranch *most of the way back, because it fit how she felt about Sam—how she knew she'd always feel.*

Megan returned to the office but struggled to concentrate on work. She remembered how strongly she felt about Sam on that trip and so many times before and after. When had she forgotten that feeling of being head over heels with excitement around him, loving every minute with him, and, most of all, certain that wherever Sam was, that's where she wanted to be?

One thing was certain—Sam had never forgotten, not one instant.

15

Day 15

MEGAN CAME home from her weekly aerobics class, hot, sweaty, and miserable. She should be out walking with Sam or going on a bike ride. They'd go hiking or out in his kayaks. Or maybe it would be time for a run. She hated exercise class and being stuck indoors. Who was she kidding? She hated exercise, period.

An escape, any kind of escape, was all she wanted at that moment. How eerie then that Sam anticipated what she needed once again. A DVD of *The Wizard of Oz,* a bucket of popcorn—freshly popped—and a soda sat on her top step. Perfect except for one problem; there was no one to share the popcorn with or the fun of one of her all-time favorite movies.

Her days of surprises from Sam were dwindling, and she wanted to make them stretch. She took a shower, put on her PJs, took care of odds and ends around the house, and settled herself on her bed for her movie night. But before she could begin, she knew she had one thing she must do. She had to re-read the note; the notes meant as much, if not more, because they saw inside her heart.

> *Dear Meg,*
>
> *You like Dorothy. I like the flying monkeys. We have our shared tradition,*

*either way. That's what matters. The end
of the movie gets us every time. "There's
no place like home." You're home for me,
and I'm home for you.*

Sam

Megan watched their favorite movie from beginning to end by herself, but in her mind, she was watching it year after year, with Sam. They would snuggle close, laugh at the silliest parts, pretend to be scared because he was too tough for the witch—not! The magic when Dorothy stepped from black and white to color—priceless. One time in particular stood out.

It was just after the holidays during Meg's third year of college, and she couldn't stand being away from Sam any longer. Somehow, it had been easier when he was attending college as well. It was true that misery loved company when they were both suffering from homesickness and being apart. Now Sam was finished; he'd doubled up on classes and completed his master's degree.

He'd found work right after graduation. It wouldn't be long before he took a leap of faith to start his own company. In the meantime, he was extremely busy, and although he missed Megan terribly, at least he was surrounded by friends, family, and work that he loved.

Sam was moving on, and Megan was stuck. She sat alone in her dorm room and stared out into a stormy night, feeling completely lost, struggling to do her studies, and wondering why she bothered if it meant being apart from everything she loved. She simply couldn't stand it. She picked up the phone and punched in the one number she knew she always could call.

"Hello?" A low voice answered, slurred with weariness. It was eleven o'clock, and Sam had hit the bed early to be up at five.

"Sammy . . . Please come and get me. I don't want this anymore. I just want to come home and be with you. I'm so lonely!"

Meg's voice broke on the last, and she let go of the tears that she had been holding back. "I don't need to be here anymore! I need you!"

Sam sat up straight and rubbed the sleep out of his eyes. He glanced at the clock and was out of bed, already pulling on jeans and a t-shirt. "I'll be there as soon as I can. Hang in there and don't cry, Meggie. You know I can't stand it when you do." His voice rough with emotion, he quickly said goodbye and headed out into the storm.

Three hours later, after a white-knuckle drive that usually took half as long, Sam stood in the lobby of Meg's dormitory. He was covered with snow and shivering even though the distance from the parking lot was not far. Megan hurried down from her room; she'd been frantic when it took him so long to get there. She burst into the lobby and flung her arms around him. "I was so worried! I'm sorry I made you come out in this terrible weather. I'm an idiot. Come up to my room, and I'll make you something hot to drink. You look like a snowman!"

Sam rested his head on top of hers and held her for a moment, inhaling the sweet scent of her hair and enjoying her warmth. Their separation was equally hard for him to deal with, but he put up a brave front for Meg's sake, knowing it wouldn't last much longer. Times like this, when he had her close, made it really difficult. What he wouldn't give to run off with her, marry her, and make her his own. He'd work three jobs to take care of her; it didn't matter. They had to wait, see what the plan was, God's plan, because human plans generally didn't usually work out. "Don't worry about making me come out in the weather. I've always told you that whenever you needed me, I'd be there, and here I am. I'll take you up on that drink. My toes are frozen from walking through the drifts. It's a real Nor'easter out there."

They went up to her room, keeping their voices down and footsteps quiet in consideration of anyone who was sleeping like they should be. Megan started her hot pot and had two steaming cups of hot cocoa within minutes, while Sam slipped off his boots, wet coat, gloves, and climbed onto her bed. They sat cross-legged across from each other and sipped their drinks. When his teeth finally stopped chattering, Sam set down their cups and pulled her into his lap. "Are you going to tell me what led to the meltdown tonight?"

Megan looped an arm around his neck and nestled her head against his chest; she felt like a little kid again, giving in to homesickness. It didn't seem so terrible now that Sam was here. "I kept thinking about the holidays, Mom, Dad, and you. The rest of my time in college seems like forever. I don't think I can wait another year and a half. It's too hard, Sammy. I want to come home and be with you. I can work in your office when you have your business. We'll be a team."

Sam rubbed her back, his large hand comforting as it circled round and round. He'd love nothing more than to have her with him now. They could marry and be together all the time, at work and at home. It was very tempting, and yet he knew it was wrong to encourage her to give up what she had started. "Meggie, you know I'd like nothing better, and I will welcome you with open arms at any business of mine, but we have to consider a few things. First, I'm not quite ready to start out on my own. I want to do that right so I can provide the best for you. Second, if we're going with that plan, we need to arrange a wedding first because I'm old-fashioned and I want to do things the way our parents did. I have a strong feeling that your father would agree with me. Third, you've worked hard to get this far, and you're almost done. I'd never forgive myself if you ended up regretting the choice to give up your education for me. Think about it, Meg. I know you can be impulsive sometimes. This is definitely not a choice you want to make on the spur of the moment. The only way we are going to last is by thinking things through and making sure each of us is happy."

The room became silent, the beating of Sam's heart against her ear the only sound. Megan reached deep inside herself for her answer and knew Sam was right. She didn't want to disappoint her parents by quitting, nor did she want to give up on her own dream. She enjoyed studying to be a paralegal even though writing would have been her first choice in her career. Her legal expertise could help Sam some day; it could also lead to becoming a lawyer if she ever wanted more. She tilted her head until she could see his sweet, brown eyes staring down at hers, patient as a saint. "You're right. I know you're right, but that doesn't make it any easier. Can you stay a while to make it easier to make it until the next break?"

Sam reached out and turned out the light then pointed out the window. The snow was coming down even harder, so hard in fact that the building across the street couldn't be seen. "I'm not going anywhere in that. You're stuck with me. Tell the resident assistant that I'm moving in."

Come next morning, a snow emergency cancelled classes at the college and closed the roads, shutting down Sam's workplace back home; most of the state had been hit hard by the storm. They made the most of their time, going for walks and snowball fights, eating at the campus cafeteria together, and getting one more night together before the roads opened and Sam had to go. It was hard to see him leave, but Megan knew he was only a phone call away.

Megan glanced at the phone, her fingers itching to pick it up. He was still only a phone call away. She came close but didn't give in. There were only five days left. She had to give him his five days. It didn't mean she'd stop thinking about all the memories he'd brought back. This plan of Sam's, it was definitely working on her. Her insides were a tangle, and her head was a mess; nothing was clear anymore except for one fact: she had five more days to think about him and what to do.

Day 16

THE AIR WAS changing, getting colder, and the leaves were starting to fall. The geese sent out their call early in the morning and in the evening as the days grew shorter. All were signs that winter was near. Usually, this was Sam's favorite time of year. Vermont was in its glory, bursting with color, inviting people to take hikes, scenic drives, or go out on the water.

Sam should have been enjoying himself but instead felt more and more unsettled; the unfamiliar uncertainty of his future was wearing him down. He found himself running—running in the early morning hours because he couldn't sleep, his mind constantly churning through his years with Meg. He barely made it through the day at work, uncharacteristically short with his staff, impatient with Michael, and procrastinating with clients, something he never did. No good for anyone, he chose to leave early and head to the woods of his childhood, where he and Megan had spent many happy hours.

He set off at a good pace, pushing himself to be on the move, rather than to take in the view. However, the further he walked, the slower his steps became as the past took over. Everywhere he turned, she was there . . . on their scavenger hunts, on countless picnics, up in a tree, playing hide and seek, or running with her golden retriever, Cookie.

Sam found their old hideaway, a spot where a fallen tree was propped against a rock. He sat down underneath it and bowed his head to his knees, giving himself a moment to let the memories take him. There was no getting Megan Taylor out of his head. *God, I need a little help here. Please, get me through this.* Slowly, he felt some peace settle in, begin to soothe him. No matter how brief a reprieve, it was enough. He began the walk back to his truck, this time taking notice of the incredible scenery around him, highlighted by the setting sun. It was a fire in the sky, rekindling the fire in his soul, and that fire's name was Meg.

The road carried him home in time to find his next little reminder for Meg, drop it off, and return. He lit his outdoor fireplace, pulled up a chair, opened a beer and stared into the flames for a long time. Sam even gave in to another beer, waited until the fire completely died, and went to bed. A third beer tempted him, but he didn't do it, hoping two would be enough to stop his mind from running again. One night. He just wanted to sleep all the way through one night and get closer to the end . . . or would it be a beginning?

MEGAN ALSO spent a day that felt like she was spinning her wheels. Nothing seemed to get accomplished, and her mind kept going in circles, second-guessing herself, her decisions, and what she was doing with her life. She was so aggravated and discouraged, she bought a quart of ice cream and ate the whole thing on her way home. Thoroughly disgusted with herself, she stormed inside and flung the container in the garbage then stood frozen at the sight on her kitchen table.

One small light sat on the table; it resembled an artificial, wax candle and dimly illuminated a framed photograph of Cookie, her first dog. A white rose was propped against it along with her note. She sank into the chair, stroking the picture as she read.

> *Dear Meg,*
>
> *Remember all of those walks, runs, and swims with Cookie? I loved how she was the first to greet us every day when we got off the bus from school. I know how much you miss her. Not to bribe you or anything, but I'll get you any kind of dog you'd like.*
>
> *Sam*

Tears ran down Megan's nose, trickled into her mouth, had her scrubbing a hand over her face. That was a lowdown move from Mr. O'Malley. Playing the sympathy card, was he? It made her start ticking off types of dogs. If he was buying, she'd better make it good. A Saint Bernard? How about a Great Dane? No, a Bermese Mountain dog! That was one offer that might tip the scales.

That night, Megan curled up in bed, thinking of Cookie, and of Sam.

16

Day 17

SAM COULDN'T sleep *again* that night and was beginning to wonder what the hazards were that went along with prolonged sleep deprivation. One might think that there would be no dreams without sleep. However, that assumption would be wrong; he spent his wide-awake hours dreaming. Ever the optimist, his mind continued to create a future with Meg, even if it was not meant to be. Sam couldn't imagine continuing to dream without her.

Morning came, still with no respite from his state of mind. Sam went for a run, showered, and headed to work. He went through the motions of his day then stopped in a gift shop in town. The diner had become off limits; Gina was too perceptive. Her radar was turned up; if Sam came in now, he'd break down, and the secret of his and Meg's estrangement would be all over town by morning. Best to be alone.

The drive to Meg's was unmemorable. The trip home was unremarkable. The evening news was unmentionable, filled with depressing and terrifying events. Sam crawled in to bed that night, once again searching his thoughts for clues to what had changed between him and Meg in the past couple of years. Three more days. He had to make it through three more days of torture. Then what? A life of black, white, and gray with no chance of color to brighten his days.

MEGAN SLAMMED the door when she arrived home. There was no sign of the day's gift from Sam. She kicked off her shoes in the hallway and went straight to the couch with her take-out dinner. It was Chinese; she'd bought Chinese on the same night Sam would, because it made her feel better, like comfort food.

What a hypocrite! She turned on the television and flicked through hundreds of channels, but nothing caught her attention. Nothing interested her anymore, not her favorite foods, not her favorite movies, not her favorite books. Her only conclusion—she'd truly enjoyed these things only when she was with Sam.

Evenings before her disaster—there was no other word for it—had been much different. Most nights were spent with Sam. He loved to cook and would dabble in her kitchen if she felt like staying home. They alternated at Sam's house on other evenings, where he'd cook inside or out; they could curl up by an indoor or outdoor fireplace either way, depending on the weather or season. Sometimes, they grabbed their favorite takeout on the way home, or he surprised Meg. Meg was a passable cook and getting better; she should be practicing to wow him now.

Occasionally, Sam would have a guy's night with Michael and some buddies from work. He might get home too late and wouldn't want to disturb Meg. Otherwise, he never tired of spending time together; he actually craved more. At the same time, girls' nights were considered par for the course, and he didn't complain. Megan had been the one to want her space from time to time, and Sam respected that.

Now she hated being alone and questioned why she

had ever been resentful. The take-out boxes were empty, and the late night shows were about to begin. Her hand almost picked up the phone to call him. It was time go to bed and attempt to find increasingly elusive sleep. She was just climbing under the covers when something caught her eye over her bed. A delicate, shimmering dream catcher made out of silver hung on the wall. A note rested on her pillow.

> *Dear Meg,*
>
> *They say this dream catcher will catch your good dreams and let all the bad thoughts drift away. Remember all the times we talked about each other's dreams? I want to know what your dreams are, now. And when they changed. Just tell me, Meg. Trust me.*
>
> *Sam*

The dream catcher glinted in the moonlight when she turned off her lamp. She didn't know how long she stared up at it before her dreams carried her back to a long ago memory.

It was Meg's senior year in high school and the night of her second prom with Sam. They had walked outside the dance hall to a gazebo that overlooked a small lake. No one else intruded; they had it completely to themselves. Sam held her in his arms, and they swayed back and forth to the music drifting softly on the air. The night was clear, the stars bright. Geese made ripples on the water as the moon reflected off its surface. No one could ask for a better night.

"It looks like you could bend over and scoop the moon out of the pond," Sam whispered, unwilling to break the peaceful atmosphere.

Meg smiled up at him, happy to be with him and have him

next to her again; he'd been away at college two years. Two to go. At least it was summer break. She wished tonight could last forever. "I bet you could have anything you ever wished for if you figured out how to catch the moon."

Sam bent over the railing of the gazebo but couldn't reach. He would've fallen in, but Megan pulled him back, both of them laughing uncontrollably at his close call. They sat together on the bench and held hands, quiet settling between them. Sam wanted badly to catch the moon and make his wish come true—to always have this sweet girl by his side and never have to be apart again. He'd only been home a short time from college. Another two years away would be agony, only made worse by the fact that Megan would have two years after that. He closed his eyes and tried to shut out those thoughts. They had to enjoy the time they had together. Their college years wouldn't last forever although it felt like it now.

"Sammy, what are your dreams for the future?" Meg's voice was soft, a little shaky. She'd been thinking about their time apart as well. It had been so much harder since Sam was not just a house away.

"Aww, Meggie. I've told you my dreams many times. They're all for you. You don't need to hear them again. It's time to think about making your dreams come true and your future now." He dropped a kiss on the top of her head, a blessing for good times to come and God to watch over this gift.

"Tell me again," she pleaded and looked up so she could see his eyes, flashing in the moonlight.

Sam met her gaze and pressed a hand to her cheek. "I'll tell you again even though you know it by heart because you helped to build my dreams. I'm going to finish school and come back to build. I'll work hard, have my own business one day, and be an architect. We'll build a home together, a life, and of course, a family. Now tell me your dreams."

Megan took his hand from her cheek and kissed his palm. "I'll go to school to be a paralegal."

"What about being a writer, Meg?"

She looked away for a long time, her face pensive. "I haven't told you this before, Sammy, but . . . I've been sending out some stories I've written."

"Meg, that's great!"

"No, it's not. So far, I've gotten enough rejections to paper every wall in a large room."

"So?"

"I need to get serious. Mom and Dad always worry about money. I guess that's part of my personality, too. I want to have a good job."

"I'll make enough money."

She shook her head. "I'm not good at being useless. Besides, maybe I can go on from being a paralegal. Become a lawyer. And someday I'll write books on the side."

"I don't know, Meg. Are you sure?"

She nodded. "I won't forget about writing. That's a fantasy; maybe I'll take the world by storm and be famous! But right now, I want to get back home as soon as I can to be with you. I wish it could happen right now."

Sam pulled her close. "Me too, Meggie, but I won't take your education away just because I'm selfish. You need to have your time. We'll be together before you know it, and then it will happen. All good things come to those who wait."

Megan woke up with a start and sat up in the darkness. Six years had gone by since she finished college. She and Sam had grown even closer in that time, worked, and matured. Except for living together under the same roof, they were as good as married. They'd been on the verge of getting engaged when Dad O'Malley died. Everything changed so quietly, so subtly, that she wasn't sure why, or how.

She was sure of this much: the change she needed didn't involve changing the man in her life; it meant changing the direction her life was taking. It was time to stop grumbling about what was wrong, figure out what was right, and make a decision about what to do next.

Day 18

THE DAY PROMISED to be a cold one. Sam could see his breath as he set out to church that Sunday morning. Usually, the fall colors took his breath away, but today he didn't even notice; his mind was too full. Besides, the chill meant the leaves would be down soon, winter would be here to stay, and his time was almost up. The thought of the long, bitter months without Meg in his life was almost more than he could take.

Sitting in the pew by his mother, surrounded by the people of his town, he went through the motions of church. An hour was spent visiting with his mother and others for coffee, an empty hour, staring off and having to beg forgiveness for his rudeness when he didn't respond to conversations. Sam begged out of dinner with his mother, something he'd seldom done since Dad's death. It was therapy for both of them, unfair of him to leave his mother hanging. Regardless, he wouldn't be good company and wasn't up to the effort of faking it.

The annual fall festival was in full swing as Sam drove into town. It pulled at him, bringing back his childhood. Hoping it might help to take his mind off his troubles but not confident that anything would work, he joined his neighbors in the festivities. The parking lot at the local supermarket was sectioned off for the numerous tents and booths set up with wares from various members of the community. The colors were bright, the air filled with the scent of apples and other good things to eat, buzzing with excitement and activity.

Sam let himself be drawn in and wandered from

table to table. There was cider and apple pie from Gina; he avoided her nosy questions but bought a mug of the spicy, hot beverage and moved on before she could pursue him. Fried dough smelled good; Megan loved the treat, always looking like she had a beard of powdered sugar when she ate it. Pumpkins of all shapes and colors filled a cart, scarecrows were propped everywhere, and wood crafts abounded, painted for all seasons. People were shopping for Christmas gifts already.

A vendor that had come in from Maine was selling beautiful paintings of the seashore along with a collection of shells. Sam picked up a white conch shell tinted a pale pink inside. He held it to his ear, and the sound of the sea reminded him of the beach trip to Maine when he and Meg were kids.

Meg was 12, Sam was 14. They were on a family vacation together with the Taylors; Sam had practically burst with excitement when he was invited. He'd never been to Maine, and the thought of spending a week with Megan just sent him over the top. Her family was like an extended version of his own family. Too bad Mom and Dad couldn't come, but maybe they were having a vacation of their own back home.

It had been an amazing week in Bar Harbor. They had gone sightseeing, out on a boat, been on a whale watch, and spent some of every day on the beach. Their cottage was on the seashore, the sound of the waves was their lullaby at night and soothing in the morning. That music of the waves, it left a mark on his soul, made him crave it, came back in his dreams long after they left.

It was their last night. After swimming most of the day, they'd spent hours combing the beach. Megan had just bent down to pick up a shell that shimmered like a rainbow. Sam stood a short distance away, looking out to sea, then turned and saw her silhouette against the sunset. He didn't know what made him do it, but when Megan turned to him, he was next to her.

He leaned in and gave her a fleeting kiss, just a brush of the lips. Felt a strange twisting in his stomach, almost like he was sick, but it felt good too. He pulled back, eyes wide; Meg's were even wider. She didn't say anything, just handed him the shell and closed his fingers around it. It was their first kiss.

Looking back, Sam wondered was that when they took their first step toward becoming something more? Or had it been on that first day when Sam raided his mother's rose garden and gave Megan his heart? He shook off the memory. The woman at the stand was staring at him oddly. It was best not to stand there any longer. He bought the shell and moved on.

Nothing else held his attention. He was aggravated with himself. Everything that used to give him pleasure was colorless and tasteless now. He had told himself he wouldn't put his life on hold for Meg, especially since he didn't know if this twenty-day interlude would work, and here he was, acting like the walking dead. Who was he kidding? Without Meg, he wasn't living. Friends and neighbors stopped briefly to chat and moved on. In a sea of people, he felt like a deserted island.

With a wrench of his heart, his thoughts turned to his mother. He had a much better understanding of what she had endured when his father died. How crushing to lose the one she loved so suddenly, without warning, permanently. And yet this business with Meg—in some ways it was even worse, because she could choose to walk away, and he would have to live with knowing she was still out there, with someone else. Whether she stayed in Cordial Creek or went around the world, the thought of her with another man would kill him. He agreed with her about one thing—they knew everyone in town, and no one else held any attraction for him, here.

He picked up some pretty stationary, a tumble of fall leaves scattered on a page. A pricking in the back of his head, that uncomfortable feeling of being watched, had him glancing behind him. No one in particular caught his notice. He bought the stationary then went to his truck to compose his next note.

He was contemplative on the trip to Meg's, trying to come to terms with the notion that God was leading him down this path. He could only wonder where God was leading Meg. Turning down her driveway, he saw that her car was there.

Should he leave the gift or knock on the door, let her invite him in? He got out of the truck, took long, slow steps to her porch, then stood with his hand against the door. Every part of his being longed to step inside, look at her, hold her, listen to her say what he wanted to hear.

He raised a hand, ready to knock. It took all he had to set the gift bag down, turn, and drive away. He didn't look back. He didn't see her step outside, a hand raised to wave and call him back to her.

MEGAN HAD BEEN to the festival with Sophie. They walked through the stands, ate candy apples and popcorn, bought a few things, and talked about inconsequential things. At one point, Megan had the strongest urge to turn around. Sophie had gone to find a bathroom. Meg looked over her shoulder and saw Sam, standing at one of the booths across the lot. His shoulders were slumped; people brushed by him with no effect, his dark eyes were lost.

It was so out of character; Sam was a people-person and knew everyone in this town. To let them wash over him like an ocean instead of riding the waves with them made her miserable. It hurt to look at him and not be able to touch him. He held something in his hands while he stared unseeingly over the crowd. It lasted only a moment, then he visibly shook himself, made a purchase, and strode away.

Megan wanted to follow him, but Sophie returned, noticing her line of sight. "Hey, isn't that Sam? Why don't you go talk to him?" Sophie had never seen anyone as devoted as Meg's other half or the kind of happiness they shared; from the moment she'd met the two of them when she moved to town in the ninth grade, it was obvious—they were soulmates.

Sophie was tiny—only five feet tall—a little plump and red-haired with shocking green eyes; she reminded people of a gypsy and was filled with fire. She used some of that flame on her best friend, turning up the heat in her words and poking her none too gently in the ribs. "What the hell is the matter with you, Meg? Get over there before you lose him."

Megan turned to Sophie, filled with confusion. "I can't right now. Listen, I'm sorry, but I'd like to go home. Will you drop me off, please?"

Sophie argued with Megan all the way to the house, a one-sided conversation to remind Megan of how lucky she was and how stupid she would be if she let Sam get away. Megan nodded in the appropriate places, made the correct sounds from time to time to show she was listening, but never cracked. She thanked Sophie, got out of the car, and walked in the house.

Megan had only been home a few minutes when once again, something from within pulled her toward her door. She stepped toward it, pressing her hand to the wood just as Sam pulled into her driveway. She peeked through the window to find him standing with his hand on the door, a mirror image on the other side. It was as if he was holding it up, or was it the other way around? She almost yanked the door open, but he turned and walked away. She hesitated only a moment then stepped out and lifted her hand. She hoped he'd see her, come back, that they could forget about everything that had happened since that Sunday drive. He didn't turn back. She was left with the kicked-up dust in the drive way, a gift bag, and an ache in her heart.

Megan didn't know how long she stood with her eyes trained on the road. With a sigh, she turned and walked inside. She pulled out the note and leaned on the kitchen counter to read it.

> *Dear Meg,*
>
> *Do you remember the seashell you gave to me at the beach in Maine? We had been picking shells for hours, trying to make our last night last forever. You told me my shell was magic. You gave it to me after you had your first kiss. Guess what? It was my first, too. You were right—that magic shell showed me a new way of looking, thinking, and feeling about you. I hope this shell is magic, too.*
>
> *Sam*

17

Day 19

NEARLY THE END of the twenty days, and Sam saw shadows of Megan everywhere. Down by the lake, curled up by the outdoor fire, sitting on the couch, by his side in the Corvette. Every time he went through town, he thought he caught sight of her figure, walking away, always walking away. At night, when he managed a restless sleep, she was there, so real that he had to shake himself until he was awake, convince him his mind was tricking him. There were much bigger problems in life, but Sam couldn't see anything except the gaping hole he was about to fall into if Megan didn't come back.

That day at work, Sam found himself holed up in his office again, unable to face others and be productive. He shoved everything off his desk, forgot about his agenda for the day, and began to sketch. Art and architectural drawings were a passion; they merged together, making many a sell when it came to helping clients to visualize their projects. He poured his soul into his drawing, pulling up every detail he could think of from his many conversations with Megan over the years. It was her dream as well as his that needed to be captured, needed to capture her heart.

MEGAN WALKED out of work and opened her car

door to find one of Sam's building sketches sitting on her dashboard with a ribbon wrapped around it and a note tucked under the bright, red satin. It was in color, rich in detail. Somehow he had taken their shared ideas, memories, and hopes for their future home and made it real. It was almost a photograph; it was that clear and descriptive. She had told him many times that he could be an artist. He was good at so many things. She stared at her gift, hard pressed to the glass picture frame, then picked up the note.

> *Dear Meg,*
>
> *This is our dream house. You've described it to me so many times. We've built it together in our minds over the years. We've made changes here and there, but this is as close as I could come to making it real. You'll have to tell me if it's right. I'll build this for you to give you your fresh start, your something new. I'll build anything for you. The Taj Mahal, the Eiffel Tower, Mount Rushmore. Tell me. Tell me what you want, tell me what went wrong, no matter how much it hurts. I can tear down a building. I can tear down what's wrong with me, with us. And build me, us, anew.*
>
> *Sam*

Day 20

SAM WAS UP before dawn, filled with a sense of panic as it came down to this, the last day. He'd put everything he had into this challenge, his heart and his soul. What if he failed? He sat on the floor in his bedroom, sifting through years of photo albums. He became frantic as he flipped through page after page. In the middle of the night, his mind touched on Meg's final gift. It had to be here!

When he didn't have any luck, he showered, dressed, and paced until it was a decent hour to show up at this mother's. He held a bag of donuts in his hand and knocked; it was still early, he wouldn't even be at work yet, but his mother was a morning person and answered the door.

"Sam! What a nice surprise. Come in and have a cup of coffee." Mare kissed his cheek and led him to the kitchen table where she placed two steaming mugs.

Her son drummed his fingers on the table and took a sip, burning his tongue. Wincing, he didn't even touch the donuts. He had neither appetite or time. "Mom, the reason I've stopped is I'm putting together a gift for Megan, and I need a picture. It's the one of us sitting on our porch steps on the first night she moved here. Do you remember it?"

He silently prayed she did, anxiety threatening to take over. No other picture—no other gift—would be acceptable. Crazy, this whole thing was crazy, but it hinged on that photograph.

She closed her eyes a moment, lost in thought. "Let me see, oh yes, I know which one. I know where it is. Just a moment." She went upstairs and took a photo album out of her dresser. She carried it down and handed it to Sam, already opened to the photograph in question. "There it is. I'll never forget that night! You two were like peas in a pod from day one."

Sam let out the breath he didn't realize he'd been holding. "Is it all right if I take it?"

Mare nodded. He searched the rest of the album. He slowed down as the pages went by, taking the time to truly study each one. "Mom, all of these are of Megan and me, from the beginning until now."

She smiled and touched his hand, her eyes soft. "It will be your wedding present . . . someday." Pure faith and love stared back at him. He prayed that she was right.

SAM MOVED FROM task to task, uncharacteristically restless and scattered. It made the rest of his staff anxious. When the others went to lunch, he retreated to his office, unable to concentrate on making conversation. Michael dropped in at the end of his own break, poking his head in the doorway to find his best friend with his elbows on his desk, hands entwined in his hair. "Hey, buddy, is there anything you want to talk about? You've been pretty hard to take, and you've got everyone walking around on pins and needles."

Sam stared at him, close to spilling everything that he'd kept inside for the past twenty days. He just couldn't do it, not so close to the end, with the outcome still unknown. "No, but thanks, anyway. I've had a lot on my mind. I'm getting away for the Columbus Day weekend. Maybe that will get my head straightened out."

Michael grinned. "I don't know if that's possible in your case, but good luck trying. Have fun, and don't come back until you're yourself again."

The clock crawled for the conclusion of the work day. Finally, unable to take it anymore, Sam wished everyone a good holiday weekend and let them go early. He hurried home to prepare. Everything had to be just right. He showered then dressed in jeans and a dark brown sweater that had been a gift from Megan because it reminded her of his eyes. He took extra care with his hair, taming the brown waves into some semblance of order even though he needed a trim. Hair kept falling into his eyes, forcing him to flick it out of the way; some gel, a gift from Meg, helped to tame it. Satisfied that this was the best he could manage, he went to Meg's and sat on her step, fighting to stay calm. The final delivery had to take place in person.

MEGAN HADN'T been able to concentrate for the entire day at the law office. She'd known for years that she disliked her job as a paralegal but suddenly it hit her: *I hate this work; it's trickling over like a poison, affecting every part of my life. I should have told Sammy I've sent out more stories I've written, gotten more rejections, have become more convinced that I'll end up being miserable in the only career I'm trained for—or someone he'll have to support if we get married.*

Was it discontentment and dissatisfaction with *herself* that was the problem and not Sam? The past nineteen days showed that she missed him, needed him, and wanted him with her, that her torment wasn't about not loving Sam anymore, but about not loving herself enough, not being worthy of Sam.

While others talked about the holiday weekend, she could only wonder what she would find on the final day of Sam's notes and gift giving. She did not share her own plans with anyone else, partially because she didn't have any, but also because she did not have any strong ties with her coworkers. That should have been a big clue regarding her unhappiness after six years of work; shouldn't they be like a family? Five o'clock seemed like it would never roll by. When it finally did, she felt mixed emotions. She was eager to discover what awaited her yet reluctant that it would be over. *I have to tell Sam the truth. That I'm not cut out to be a paralegal and may never be a writer, so then what? Yes, he'll take care of me, but that's not the partnership we've always had.*

Her spirits soared when she saw Sam on her step. All of these years passing through each other's lives, Megan had taken for granted that Sam was the best-looking man she'd ever seen. The sight of him made her melt, made it hard to breathe, put her brain on hold. Her heart started to skip as she stepped out of her car, her eyes never leaving his face.

As for Sam, he wore his heart as he looked at her, hoping to show her that no one could feel as strongly as he did in that moment. He waited until she reached the bottom step then stood up, hand out. "I thought you'd never get home."

"Me neither," she murmured and took his hand, the warmth of his touch filling an empty place deep inside. He pulled her in close, a desperate need to be near her, and she felt fine tremors running through his sturdy frame. It felt right to have him here, to be with him.

They walked inside together. She offered him a drink, but he refused, leading her to the living room to sit on the couch. He sat beside her and set her last gift on her lap.

Megan looked down to see a picture of them when they were children, sitting on the steps of the O'Malley front porch, hand in hand, with smiles that stretched wide across their faces, light in their eyes, blueberry pie stains on their clothes, and milk mustaches on their lips.

Sam held out his final note.

"Would you read it aloud?" she asked hoarsely.

He nodded.

"Dear Meg,

Do you remember when this photograph was taken? I do. I remember everything about you. It was the first night that you walked into my life. My parents invited you and your family for dessert. We sat on the porch steps, made a mess of ourselves, and swore we'd be best friends forever. Look at us! Look at our faces, look at how we held hands, look at the trust and excitement. It was all so exciting and new. We've kept the promise all these years. And no matter what happens next, we'll always be best friends.

"Somewhere along the way, Meg, you stopped loving me as more than a friend. It never stopped for me. I couldn't wait to see the something new you would do or say or be. Every minute with you in it could hold a mystery, a secret, a surprise. I've spent twenty days showing you all the little things I already know about you, but I want to spend a lifetime discovering all of the unknowns that you hold inside of you and me as well. Go away with me this weekend. Let's start over, start fresh, make it new again, like that first day we met. By the end of this long weekend, choose your future—one with me or without. Whatever you choose, I'll honor your decision, but I still hope and pray that you'll choose me. Love always, Your Sam."

Sam's voice broke on the last part, and he had to get up, move away from her, not lose control any further. He stood at the window and looked out, clearing his throat. "Just Yes or No. If it's No, I'll leave. No messy scene, I promise."

Megan studied the picture for a long time, missing the girl she used to be, so happy, carefree, and sure of herself. She'd been content then, glad to finally have ties and stop being a tumbleweed. It dawned on her, the longer she looked, that the young Sam had never changed, at heart he was the same. Yes, he'd grown older, he'd matured. Time and pain may have added shadows to his eyes, but he still was the boy who couldn't wait to see what was next in life. It didn't matter where he was or what he was doing. There were always doors to be opened and new sights to be seen.

She looked up from the picture, into those eyes she had seen so many times and saw something that had not been there before their Sunday drive. There was fear of the unknown, something he had never questioned before, but only welcomed. The unknown had stopped him cold only once before: when his father died. She had stopped him in his tracks again, put that fear there, and she didn't like it.

"Yes, I'll go." Three little words lit a spark of hope once more.

18

The Retreat

IT WAS A TWO hour drive yet felt like the road stretched on forever. They opened with small talk—a first for Megan and Sam. Being best friends forever had meant endless fuel for conversation or not having to say anything at all. Now an awkward silence fell after the topics of the weather and work had been exhausted. The ease they had always shared was missing, which made sitting side by side difficult.

Sam felt as if he'd said it all—anything that mattered anyway—in the past twenty days. It was Megan's turn to pick up where they left off. Her turn to salvage their relationship if that was her intention. Or let it sink.

For Megan, it was as if a wall had sprung up between them, a barrier of her own making that she did not know how to tear down. She wanted to discuss the many memories Sam had given back to her, the gifts that had touched her heart. At the same time, she was afraid, afraid that once she began, she would be buried under an avalanche of their past.

It was a great relief when Sam stopped at a ranger station to double check on his directions. There were twenty minutes left on the twisting and turning maze of a mountain road. It brought them to a rustic cabin, tucked in the shore of a small lake in northern Vermont. There were no neighbors, no signs of civilization. Their only company was wildlife, towering pines, water like glass and an amazing sunset.

Sam opened Meg's door, something he had never tired of. "A lady is meant to always be treated like a lady," echoed in Meg's mind, her eyes following his back as he walked away.

He stood tall and straight, strong enough to carry the world. He easily managed the task of carrying their bags. He bowed his head for Megan to precede him up the slate steps and told her huskily, "Ladies first."

There was hope burning in his eyes, so bright she felt it stirring inside of her. She pushed the heavy door open and walked into a fairy tale. It was a beautiful log cabin, the color of the wood inside warm and inviting. Cozy and intimate, it was tiny with only a kitchenette, a small living room area, and a loft with a large bed and bathroom. A table set for two sat by a picture window overlooking the lake. Someone had been there a short time before their arrival; dinner was warming in the oven, candles were lit on the table, a bottle of wine stood beside two wine glasses, and a fire crackled and popped in the stone fireplace.

Megan turned to Sam, awestruck and without words. He took her coat, keeping his thoughts to himself, though he wore his strong emotions on his face. They had gone away together many times but never to any place as special as this. "Sammy, this is incredible. I wouldn't be surprised if a white horse turned up at my door with Prince Charming asking for directions. Thank you so much for doing this, for everything." For twenty years . . .

"You're welcome. I hoped you'd like it. I searched for days for the perfect spot." *Nearly twenty days*, Sam was thinking. His internet searches had finally made a hit yesterday. It left him only one day to make everything fall into place.

He took their bags upstairs, Megan trailing behind him, to find roses and chocolates on the pillow of a second bedroom. No assumptions. No pressure. He had spared no expense, choosing a place that attended to every detail to create a lovers' nest. Sam gave his gift and his heart went with it.

Sam returned downstairs to find Megan sitting on the sofa, fingering the intricate print on the fabric that captured a scene of the wilderness with bears, deer, fish, lakes and forest. He slowly approached, drinking her in as she was lost in thought. To see her. To have her close to him once more. He reached out to her and took her hand, kissing it and drawing her to her feet. "Come join me for dinner. You must be starved."

She obliged and allowed Sam to wait on her, a role she had usually performed for him. It made her feel good to spoil him and take care of him, but she let him do it this time. Because he wanted to. Because he needed to do it. He poured wine and stepped into the kitchenette. Dishes rattled, the oven opened and closed, and he appeared with two beautiful plates of lasagna, salad, and a basket of Italian bread.

It was Megan's favorite meal. Once again, Sam used what he knew about her to entice her. There was variety, ensuring nothing would be humdrum. Besides the typical lasagna, there was a pan of lasagna with spinach, chicken, and white sauce. They both ate hungrily; it was much later than their usual dinner hour, and nerves had kept both from eating much during the day.

Food helped the conversation to flow again. The cabin gave them a starting point with its surprises, such as the footprints of animals painted high over their heads, the deer antler chandelier, and the wooden carvings of forest animals tucked in various nooks.

There was a gradual shift to plans for the holidays, vacations that they could take, places to go. Dessert followed—again her favorite, chocolate cream pie. Sam polished it off and cleared the dishes. He was washing them in a suds-filled sink when Megan called out, "Leave them, Sam. They'll keep. Come sit with me."

It was what he had been waiting for, to be missed, to be wanted. He cleared his throat, dried his hands, mentally preparing himself. He had spent twenty days without her, the longest stretch with the exception of their college years. The thought of being close to her again had him breaking out in a cold sweat.

She was on the rug in front of the fire, feet tucked beneath her, with two wine glasses in her hands. She tipped her head up to offer him a kiss as he sat down beside her and took a glass of wine. It was tentative at first. They were both cautious, had to take it slow. "Thank you again, Sam. This is absolutely amazing."

Sam sipped slowly, regaining his composure or at least trying to find some semblance of it, after her kiss. He suddenly felt off balance, ready to spin out of control from her proximity, her touch, and her warmth. "So are you."

Megan set the wine glasses aside and wrapped her arms around Sam, giving him everything—her feelings, her past love, her turmoil—in her kiss. When she broke away, they were both breathing heavily. "That's in return for the kiss you gave me at the beginning of the twenty day challenge. I've thought about it every day since that moment when I met a Sam I'd never known before. I've wanted to give one in return ever since."

"I haven't been able to put it out of my mind either," he whispered then scooped her up into his arms. He sat down in a large recliner that felt like sinking into heaven, but he already had made it there with Megan beside him. He kissed her again, this time taking it slow, making it gentle, and going easy on her emotions. He told her without words that he was still the Sam she had always known, and yet, she would never become bored with a man like him in her life.

Meg's breath let out in a long sigh when his lips let go of hers. It felt like coming home. An empty space inside of her, one she didn't know she had, filled to overflowing. She tucked her head beneath his chin and closed her eyes, holding on to the moment, trying to make it last. Sam stroked her back, moving in gentle circles until his arm grew heavy from the heat of the fire and plain exhaustion after the past twenty days. They both drifted off.

Sometime in the night, Sam awoke. He carefully picked her up and carried her to bed, crawling in next to her as she held out her arms.

IT WAS LIKE their first night together, not long after she graduated from college and came home to Cordial Creek. Sam laid her on the bed in his house, oblivious of roses, chocolates, or the scent of apples and cinnamon in the sheets. He began to peel off her clothes, and she returned the favor, fingers fumbling in her haste. They knelt together, candlelight flickering over their bodies in a strange dance of darkness interspersed with light. It was the first time they had seen each other completely naked, the first time they completely gave themselves to each other.

They were old-fashioned, had talked about waiting for marriage, but had waited so many years already; compared to all their friends they were very late bloomers, to say the least. They had been each other's first date, had experienced their first kiss together, and now they were each other's one and only. In all their years together, there had been no others. Megan knew now, no one else could compare. They'd be each other's forever.

Sam set the roses and chocolate on the nightstand then twined his fingers in Megan's hair. He kissed her until they had to come up for air. Their hands roamed over their bodies, discovering each other again for the first time on this weekend of new beginnings.

It wasn't long before they were making love with a desperation and passion that took them beyond anything they'd ever imagined. Their bodies welcomed one another, belonged to each other, became whole. When it was over, Megan nestled under the covers in Sam's arms, no need to dress when they could keep each warm.

19

A Rude Awakening

MEGAN WAS THE first to awaken the next morning. A thick, cotton robe was conveniently placed on a hook in the bathroom. She slipped it on and tiptoed downstairs, carrying the roses from the bedroom. She put the flowers in a vase to decorate the coffee table, made breakfast from the completely stocked kitchen, and had coffee ready when Sam came down wearing a similar robe.

His eyes were still sleepy, his smile lazy, and he spoke with a voice that was low and hoarse. "'Morning, Sunshine." He slipped his arms round her and let her lean back against him.

Megan turned to kiss his cheek, a butterfly brushing on his skin. "Good morning. Go sit, and I'll bring you breakfast."

He didn't argue. She returned with a steaming cup and a loaded plate. Sam took a sip of the hot brew then pulled her into his lap. "You're spoiling me. You don't know what it's been like without your coffee all of this time. I think I've been suffering from withdrawal. Thank you."

She kissed him back then poked his nose. "You're welcome. Now eat before my hard work goes to waste when it gets cold. It's not every day I cook a real breakfast, usually only weekends, and I'll get out of it if I can."

A hearty meal of bacon, eggs, toast, sliced bananas and strawberries, and juice followed. When they had finished, they worked together in the kitchen in a companionable silence. Sam pressed a kiss to her neck when they were finished and went upstairs to shower. He returned shortly to start the fireplace once again.

Megan pensively considered what to say next as she stood at the railing of the loft, simply happy to watch him. She had gone upstairs to get dressed then became sidetracked by the sight of him. He was stop-her-in-her-tracks, catch-her-breath handsome, like a rugged mountain man. His broad shoulders filled out his green flannel shirt, and he wore jeans that fit right in all the right places. But it wouldn't have mattered what Sam wore, because he was comfortable in his own skin. He had always known exactly where he was going and where he was meant to be. It was Megan who had somehow become lost along the way.

Sam sat down in front of the fire, arms resting loosely on drawn-up knees as he watched the pictures in the flames. Megan walked down the stairs and dropped down beside him, her eyes somewhere far away. He took her hand and waited until she looked at him, could see nothing but pure honesty in his eyes. "I love you. You know that. Whatever's wrong, I'll fix it. I think it's clear that you still love me."

"Yes. I do. Sam, that was never the problem . . ."

"Answer one question for me, and everything else will fall into place later. All right?"

"Sam, you're trying to simplify things, but I need to talk about who I am and why I feel . . ."

"Will you marry me? Yes or no."

"Sam! I can't answer that. Not until you've listened

to . . ."

"You have doubts."

"Yes, but not the kind you think . . ." She broke off when she saw the expression on Sam's face and wished she could pull the words back into her mouth. She raised a hand to stop the train wreck, but it was too late.

Sam didn't give her a chance to explain herself. He grabbed his coat off the peg by the door, strode outside, and slammed the door hard enough to make the cabin shake, leaving Megan behind him.

TUCKED IN THEIR cozy getaway, neither Sam nor Megan had paid attention to the early snow that began to fall. It didn't even register that while a storm was brewing inside, a bigger one was about to be full-blown outside. Sam was only fifty feet away from the cabin when the wind kicked up and began blowing the snow, taking away visibility.

A little ways in, a glance over his shoulder, and the cabin was gone. Good! Best to get lost right now and never come back. He forged on into the woods, not caring or even feeling the cold, he was so angry. He had spent twenty days consumed with keeping Megan in his life only to be told she was still uncertain. His anger built until his head was pounding. It took at least twenty minutes of tromping in the snow before the biting cold began to work on him and he started to question the sanity of his present course.

He couldn't see anything in front of him in the white-out conditions. He continued on, unwilling to turn back until he cooled off if that were remotely possible. The anger, bubbling inside, was frightening; it had to be extinguished before facing Megan again.

Suddenly, where there had been solid ground, there

was only air. He didn't know how far he dropped until he landed with a sickening crunch. He groaned with the explosion of pain in his left leg. Sam looked down, still unable to see much of anything. He was lying in a crumpled heap in the snow. He reached down and felt his thigh, hissing when he touched a hard bump that sent him reeling. He held up shaking fingers covered in something warm and wet. Bright, red blood was startling, dripping onto the white canvas of the snow.

Damn it! Not only had he been stupid to march off into the unknown in a storm, unprepared with all the necessary gear, now he had gone and hurt himself. Cool off—ha! He was about to freeze to death. He had to be more careful what he wished for.

Sam pulled up the hood of his coat then fumbled with his belt and pulled it off. Next order of business—sitting up. He took deep breaths and pulled himself into a sitting position. With a trembling hand, he pressed down on his thigh. It was the bone, just beneath his jeans, a jagged end poking out of his skin. He had to stop the bleeding. He wrapped the belt above the wound and tightened as hard as he could with hands that were growing numb. Mercifully, he blacked out and fell back onto the snow.

MEGAN PACED back and forth in the cabin. When an hour went by and Sam didn't return, she couldn't stand it anymore. She grabbed Sam's hat and gloves and headed out in the direction he had taken. The snow and wind had wiped away all signs of his path. She had to find him, to finish what she was going to say to him. It wasn't Sam that she was questioning but what she wanted to do with her life. The one thing she was sure of was that she wanted, no needed, him in it.

She trudged through the snow, beginning to shiver. She was scared; if she was chilled already, imagine how Sam felt. She had no idea where she was headed, but something tugged on her, made her go in one direction with a growing sense of need. After twenty minutes of walking, she started to call his name. "Sam! Samuel O'Malley, you answer me! Please, Sam!" She called out, her voice breaking in desperation.

His voice came faintly from a short distance away. "Down here, and for God's sake, Meg, be careful. There's a drop."

It felt like hours until she reached his side and threw herself down beside him. "Sammy! Oh, Sammy, no!" She cried out when she saw the blood spreading out over the snow beneath his body.

He looked up at her with torment in his eyes, teeth chattering, but tried to smile. "You always said I could be a stubborn idiot. Well, I've gone and done it this time. My leg's broken, and I can't go anywhere." His eyes closed, and he rested his head in the snow. He was shaking uncontrollably from the cold and shock, his face as white as the snow that fell around them.

Megan pulled his hat out of her pocket and put it on his head then slipped on his gloves before yanking off her jacket and covering him with it. His eyes fluttered open, his words beginning to slur. "No, Meg, not your jacket. You need it."

She bent down and kissed him, blinking back tears. "Nonsense—you need it more than I do. I've got plenty of other clothes on. Look at me, I'm bundled like the time your mother taught you to ride a bike without training wheels. You had so many coats on you could hardly move. We laughed to look at you." Megan grabbed his hand and gave it a hard squeeze. He was slipping away from her; she could see his eyes beginning to fade. "You listen to me, Samuel O'Malley. I am going for help, and you had better damned well be here when I get back, because you didn't let me finish what I had to say in the cabin." Tears started to slip from the corners of her eyes and fell on his face.

Sam lifted a trembling hand to her cheek. "Don't cry, Meg. I'll be here . . . Before you go, gotta stop . . . the bleeding. The belt's loose . . . gotta pull it tight." Bleeding? Why was there bleeding? What had he gotten himself into, and how could she get him out?

Mega saw his makeshift tourniquet. That and the cold had combined to keep him from bleeding to death, but blood continued to flow. She took off her own belt and slid it underneath his leg, making him grunt with the movement. Meg's hand brushed against the bone, out of place, abnormal. A compound fracture! The worst kind. Why here and now of all places? Sam was ripped into total consciousness when she tugged the belt with all of her strength. He clenched his teeth and bit his lip but couldn't hold back a scream when she grabbed hold of his belt as well and pulled it tight against the wound that was a fire in his thigh.

Megan leaned down and kissed him, crying freely now. "I'm sorry, Sammy. Now remember what I said and use that stubborn side of you to set your mind to hanging on. I love you with all of my heart, and I'm not letting go without a fight."

Sam held her for a moment, his eyes soft. "I'll do my best. I love you, too. You know that. Now go, before you freeze."

Megan turned and went the way she came, running faster than she ever had in her life. She followed her footprints that she could barely make out in the falling snow, the clock ticking in her mind. She thought about how long he'd been out in the cold, how long it would take to get help. It was too long. She made it to the truck, thanked God for four-wheel drive, and rocketed down the mountain. She prayed for speed, for the truck to stay on the road, for God to be with Sam. She cried in relief at the sight of the ranger station, nearly jumped out of the truck before it stopped moving, and ran inside.

No stranger to emergencies, Paul Johnson was out of his chair the moment he saw Megan's face; her fear was written all over it without saying a word. He wore a full, blond beard, hair on the long side, brushing his collar, and was a big, solid man. He made Megan think of Grizzly Adams from the television show of long ago. She hoped he was a strong enough to carry her burden.

"I need your help. My boyfriend fell and broke his leg in the woods. He has a compound fracture, and he's probably suffering from hypothermia." *Please help me to help him. Please help me to save him. Please help me to save myself.* The words were a jumble to the ranger, to herself, to God.

Paul turned to his phone and dialed. "How long ago did it happen?" He asked as he waited for someone to answer. Damn storm! It was slowing everything down. What would they do it they couldn't get the paramedics? Carry him out themselves.

BY THE TIME they reached Sam, his skin was tinged with blue and he was shaking violently from the cold. Megan took his hand. "Sammy, help is here. This is Ranger Paul Johnson. Paramedics are on the way to get you out of here."

Paul was already putting another tourniquet on Sam's leg then wrapping blankets around his body. Sam's eyes slowly opened. "Thank you," he whispered to the stranger. His eyes found Meg. "I . . . d-d-did what you . . . told . . . me . . . to."

Megan smiled at him even though she was crying. "Good. Now keep on doing it." She squeezed his hand and touched her forehead to his. "Look at me, Sammy. You stay with me. Here and now, stay with me. There can't be an *us* without you in the picture."

Paul poured a steaming cup of coffee. "We need to bring up his body temperature. Please hold his head so he can drink this." Megan cradled Sam's head while the ranger slowly tipped the hot liquid into his mouth. When the ranger was satisfied that he'd had enough, he pulled heat packs out of his first aid kit and set them all over Sam's body beneath the blankets. Shaking. He was shaking, uncontrollably, gasping with the pain in his leg.

Minutes later, the paramedics arrived. Speed was of the essence. They lifted Sam onto a stretcher with Megan holding on as if for life—it could be Sam's life—and Sam blacked out.

20

Putting the Pieces Back Together Again

MEG SAT IN A hospital waiting room praying for Sam, who had gone into surgery two hours ago. She stood as Michael and Mare O'Malley ran down the hallway, eyes only on her. Michael reached her first and scooped her into his arms. "Any word about Sammy?"

She shook her head. Mare hugged her fiercely. "He'll be all right. He's an O'Malley. He's made of a stronger mettle than most."

They sat down together, a trio who loved Sam more than anyone else in the world, trapped in a waiting game. Mare sat with her eyes closed, silently praying. She'd lost her husband much too soon; the possibility of losing Sam was one she could not fathom. Parents were not meant to outlive their children.

Michael touched Mare's hand. "How about a cup of tea?" She managed a small smile and a nod. He turned to Meg. "You, too?"

Megan accepted his offer then took Mare's hand. She was not certain if it was to lend her own or to borrow the older woman's strength. "I'm so sorry, Mom. That phone call was the hardest one I've ever had to make."

Mare squeezed her hand in return. "I'm just so glad you were with him, Megan. You're everything to him."

Michael returned with the drinks. "Meg, tell me

again. I don't understand how it happened."

She had not given details on the brief call to Sam's mother. She had put it off as long as possible but couldn't avoid the truth when she was face to face. "Sam and I went to a cabin in the mountains for the long weekend, for a romantic getaway."

Michael motioned for her to stop. "What has been going on with you two? I haven't seen you with Sam in nearly a month, and he didn't say anything about taking you with him. That's really unlike Sam. He usually tells me everything when it comes to you because he doesn't feel like it needs to be a secret."

Megan closed her eyes, silently thanking Sam for her privacy. Had he been protecting her or himself? It didn't matter. Once again, he had stood up to the test. It was her turn now. "Sam and I took a little break. It wasn't anything Sam did. It was all me. I've been going through an ... identity crisis. I started questioning everything about my life, even Sam. At the end of our break, we took this weekend to talk about the future."

Mare slowly sipped her tea, choosing her words carefully. "I knew something wasn't right when I didn't see you at church or Sunday dinners. Sam wouldn't talk to me about you either, something that has never happened before. Usually, he just spills over with news about you; he just can't help himself."

At that uneasy moment, Sam's surgeon, a white-haired man in glasses, approached their group. "Excuse me, are you all here for Sam O'Malley? I'm Dr. Richardson."

"How is my son, Dr. Richardson?" Mare took Michael's and Meg's hands and held on with all of her strength.

"He's in recovery. When he was brought in, he was suffering from shock, hypothermia, and severe blood loss. We had to stabilize his condition before we could operate. Once we did, we repaired a compound fracture in his upper thigh. We secured it with a steel pin. We need to monitor him for the next twenty-four hours for the possibility of infection. He's in critical but stable condition, badly weakened from the conditions, injury, and surgery."

Mare clung to Megan and Michael's hands, forcing herself to stay calm. "When can we see him?"

"As soon as he is out of recovery," the doctor reassured them. He answered any questions they had then continued his rounds.

Mare stood up on legs that had become unsteady. "I need to go to the chapel." Michael and Megan walked with her, asking staff for directions, until they found the empty room. It was softly lit by the glow of stained glass and candles, peacefully quiet. Michael stopped at the doorway, his face strained, tension coursing through his body. "I'm sorry. I can't sit still right now. I've got to move. I have my cell phone if you need me." He left them to start walking the many levels of the hospital.

Mare and Megan sat side by side, praying and waiting. An hour limped by, then two until the women thought they would go out of their minds with worry. Finally a nurse approached and quietly told them Mrs. O'Malley could see her son. Mare stood to go then turned to Meg, eyes glistening with tears.

"You go and spend some time alone with him, then I'll come. Tell him I love him and that I'm not going anywhere, okay?" Megan pleaded, trying to keep her voice steady.

Mare gave her a hug and left Megan to continue praying. The stress and fear of the day got the best of her until she leaned on the pew in front of her and fell asleep.

She and Sam were walking in the woods, hand in hand, when they stopped by a large oak. Looking up, she stared at a large heart that Sam had carved with their initials. The tree truly existed. It stood halfway on the path between their houses and was one of their favorite places to visit with a wonderful shared memory of the day Sam marked his love for her.

In the dream, they stood holding hands under the heart. Sam bent to kiss her when a terrible storm hit. The sky grew dark. The wind tore at their clothes and hair, the rain pelted their skin.

There was a terrible explosion of lightning that knocked them to the ground and an ear-shattering clap of thunder. Megan clasped her hands over her ears. When she opened her eyes, the tree was split down the middle, breaking the heart and blasting their names apart. Megan turned to see Sam lying on the ground next to her, eyes closed, completely motionless. His chest no longer rose and fell, and he was completely drained of color, wax-like in appearance. "Sam! No! Oh, God, no!"

She screamed and jerked awake. Michael was standing over her, touching her shoulder. "Michael, is Sam . . . is he . . ." She couldn't bring herself to say it. What if the dream was true?

Michael's eyes softened as he saw the pain in Meg's. He took her hand. "He's asking for you."

A PALE GHOST of a figure lay on the bed, dark hair a stark contrast against his skin as it fell into his eyes and across the white pillow. Sam's left leg was elevated on a cushion, not in a cast yet, while the surgical incision healed. Monitors blipped, and I.V.'s dripped in the dimly lit room. He looked like a stranger. The true Sam O'Malley was always on the move, animated and filled with a passion for living.

Megan carefully sat on the edge of the mattress on his right side, resting her hand in his as she did. "Hey, lady." Sam's voice was a whisper, drifting up while his fingers closed with the slightest pressure on hers. His eyes opened to drink her in. He was filled with the need to see her.

"Hey, yourself. They sure have got you hooked up. When you hurt yourself, you make sure you do the job right. How do you feel?" She could've thumped herself in the head. It was obvious how he felt.

He swallowed hard, his face spasming for a brief moment while his grip tightened. "Ah . . . it's hurting. It throbs with my heartbeat. If I move at all . . . well, I try not to. They're watching everything." His eyes closed, and he fell silent. Megan thought he was asleep until she heard him speak, soft and low. "I'm sorry I put you through this."

Megan bent over him and pressed her forehead to his. "I'm the one who's sorry. I never meant for any of it to happen. You never let me finish talking this morning—"

He squeezed her hand hard again, his body tensing with a particularly sharp stab of pain. "Wait, don't tell me yet. Before you do, look me in the eye and listen to what I have to say."

Not wishing to upset him, and unable to tear her eyes away if she tried, she focused on the deep, brown eyes she hoped would meet her every morning when she woke up and be the last thing she looked at before she went to bed for the rest of her life. "Okay, let's hear it."

Sam breathed in slowly, breathed out, centering himself. He had to get this right. "Meg, you've said you were unhappy. You act as if you feel trapped or stuck. Maybe you're waiting for a sign, something big and fantastic, and you thought you needed someone new or someplace new to make that happen. That's not what life is about, Meg. It's all the little things that are around you every day, just like it's all of the little things about you that make me love you. But, if you still need something fresh and new in your life, we can make it happen . . . together. You can quit your job and do something you really love. We can move into our dream house. We can leave this town if that's what you need. We can travel, see the world. I don't care if we weave nets on a beach in Aruba or live like a Sherpa on Mount Everest. Whatever you want, it's yours, but you've got to talk to me. I can't read your mind.

"I'm asking one thing of you, Meg. Have faith in me when I tell you the one thing you don't need to change in your life is me. Trust me. You need me in your life, and I need you." His voice broke on the last.

Megan leaned forward and cupped his face in her hands. "Samuel O'Malley, you stubborn Irishman, that's what I was trying to tell you when you took off this morning. I know I want you in my life—you're the only thing I'm sure about. I knew it in my heart all along. Every day you just reminded me more about all of the little things I had forgotten.

"I'm so sorry, Sam. On that trip down the mountain, when I thought I might lose you, I realized that all my worries are tiny compared to that one. Then I dreamed that I really did. The thought of you being gone, of the choice being taken away from me, showed me you have always been and always will me my only choice. Just tell me this, Sam: if I quit my job and focus on being a fulltime wife, mother, and a writer"—her voice shook—"will you hate if I'm not great at *any* of those jobs? If I'm not your partner anymore, but turn into someone . . . helpless that you have to . . . to take care of."

His eyes widened. "Is that what scares you?"

She nodded tearfully.

"You've just spent the day saving my life. I'm laying here helpless. But I couldn't be happier. Sometimes I'll be the strong one. Sometimes you'll be the strong one. Okay?"

She drew back, blinking as she absorbed his point.

Sam laughed quietly then winced as even that shifted his leg. Meg kissed him. She could never get enough of kissing him. She took her time, making sure there would be no doubt about her sincerity. The heart monitor started to pick up its pace, making them both laugh softly. She pulled back and took his hand in hers. "There's only one way to make sure you never pull a stunt like this again. I'll just have to marry you."

Sam's eyebrows shot up, leaving him momentarily speechless while the heart monitor bleeped insistently again. "Am I delirious? Was that a proposal? I have a ring . . . though not on me at the moment. You'll have to take my word for it."

A nurse walked in, her expression and tone scolding. "Mr. O'Malley needs his rest. I'm going to have to ask you to leave."

Sam wouldn't let go of Meg's hand yet. He pulled her close for one more kiss. Megan whispered in his ear. "You already did propose. I'm saying Yes. I love you. I can wait for the ring." She stood up and headed for the door before the nurse bodily removed her.

"Love you, too," Sam called weakly after her, starting to fade. The nurse gave him a sip of water, made sure all was well, then ordered him to rest. He closed his eyes and sifted through the pictures in his mind until he pulled out the right one.

Meg was eight and Sam was ten. It was summertime, their first, glorious summer together. There were days of endless adventures and discovery. They were inseparable, "two peas in a pod," their mothers said. Some days they agreed on what to do.

If they disagreed, they would spend half the day doing what Megan wanted and the other half what Sam wanted. They were good at compromising and finding answers together. On this particular day, the first half of the day had been spent playing Robin Hood, climbing trees, hiding in the bushes, raiding their mothers' costume jewelry to steal from the rich and give to the poor.

The second half of the day was spent in Sam's tree house, playing house. Sam really didn't like to play house, and if his buddies ever found out, he would have to pound them to keep it a secret. However, Sam was a good sport and stuck to their arrangement. Even at age ten, Sam lived by his word. If Megan could be one of the Merry Men, Sam could play the father in their home sweet home.

Megan had just poured iced tea and put out cookies, wearing a cute little apron her mother made for her. Sam sat at the table, playing his part. A baby doll was wrapped in a blanket on the bed made of sleeping bags. Sam wore one of his dad's hats—the one Frankie the Snowman would later wear—and his dad's tie. He'd just started to sip his tea, fittingly out of a tea cup, when he stopped and set it down.

"Wait a minute, wait a minute. We can't start this way. Meet me out on the porch and leave your apron in here. Just give me five minutes!" With that, Sam skedaddled out the creaky door onto the boards with a railing that formed the porch, or balcony, or barricade—whatever the game of the day called for, and he scrambled down below.

Megan waited for what seemed like five minutes but was closer to two and stepped outside, holding the railing and peering around the yard. There was no sign of Sam yet.

"Meggie! Close your eyes!" He climbed like a monkey to the top, wildflowers in his teeth, panting from the exertion. He stopped in front of her. "Okay, open 'em!"

Meggie obliged to see Sam holding a bouquet of brown-eyed Susans and daisies. These weren't stolen from any gardens. "Why, thank you! They're beautiful, Sammy!" She buried her nose is them.

Sam took her by surprise again when he dropped down on one knee. He reached up and took her hand. "Meggie Taylor, will you marry me?" He winked and whispered, "Play along. If we're playin' house, we gotta get married."

Megan winked back and hugged him. "Oh, Samuel O'Malley, yes, I will marry you."

Sam smiled and tipped back his father's hat. "I thought you'd say that, so I came ready. This is for you." He pulled out one of his mother's costume rings, big and gaudy with a huge, blue stone that sparkled in the sun. "It's blue to match your eyes."

Megan held out her hand, and he slipped it on her finger. "It's the prettiest thing in the world! I'll wear it forever!"

Sam smiled to himself as he slipped into sleep. *Forever* had lasted until his mother found out about the jewelry raid and he got a spanking. It had been worth it to see Meggie light up. He wondered if his mother still had the ring.

21

Homecoming

TWO WEEKS IN a hospital bed was an eternity. Sam thought his separation from Megan was the longest torture of his life. He was wrong. Although his two-week sentence felt like it lasted forever, he was not lonely. As soon as people in Cordial Creek heard about Sam's injury, they rallied and came to visit the hospital even though it was an hour and a half away. Everyone Sam knew stopped by at some point. Some carpooled, some took the bus, some came several times.

Gina made repeat appearances with treats from the diner. "I've got to make sure you get some real food," she clucked every time she came, shaking her head at his gaunt face. Sam's employees, Dr. Harding, and the paramedics, Pete and Joe, were regulars as well. Mare and Meg shared a hotel room nearby for the duration. Michael took care of everything at the office and even came in early almost every day.

Cards, flowers, candy, and gifts filled the hospital room. Sam was embarrassed by all of the attention. He even made Megan give a lot of it to other patients with no visitors. Everyone's caring gestures and presence helped to distract Sam, yet the best medicine was Meg. She made him want to wake up every day.

Finally Dr. Richardson deemed his incision was

healed enough to put on a cast. Today Meg stood beside Sam as he sat in a wheelchair, holding his hand. Michael and Mare had brought Sam's things to Mare's car and were waiting for a hospital attendant to wheel Sam out.

Megan wore a blue sweater that complemented her eyes, jeans, and a ponytail. She looked fresh and young, the most beautiful thing Sam had ever seen.

Megan was thinking along the same lines when it came to Sam. Although he had lost weight and had lines of pain around his eyes and mouth, his face was filled with such light. It was as if a candle had been lit and was burning bright. He wore a deep green sweater, and his dark hair was shining as it tumbled across his forehead. Megan thought nothing in the world looked better than Sam at that moment.

Sam motioned to his lap. "Please sit down." Before Meg could argue, he pulled her down and hooked his arms around her.

Megan started to squirm then stopped, fearful she'd hurt him. "Doesn't my weight hurt your leg?"

He shook his head. "Nothing hurts right now, not with you here. If I can't get on one knee, this will have to be good enough." He brought up one hand to touch her cheek. "Megan Taylor, will you marry me?"

She gave him a shaky smile. "Yes, Sam. I thought we already had this settled."

He returned her smile and reached into a pocket of his pajama bottoms—the only garment loose enough to fit over the cast on his leg—then took her hand and slid a ring on her finger. It was large, gaudy, with a blue stone that made facets of light dance on the hospital walls. "When I can get up and around, I'll bring you the real one. Until then, will you accept your ring from our first marriage, twenty years ago?"

Megan could only nod as she began to cry. She bent her forehead to his. "Sammy, you are some kind of wonderful."

ONCE HOME, Michael and Mare did not linger. Sam crutched his way in. They settled him on the couch and made sure he didn't need anything. They left the lovebirds to their privacy.

That first night home, Megan slid on to the edge of the couch and held onto Sam. He smiled and tried to scooch over. "I'm sorry. You'd be a lot more comfortable upstairs."

Megan held on tighter. "I don't care. You're not going up and down those stairs. I can put up with a little discomfort after all you've been through."

Sam turned to her and kissed her with only his gentleness this time. "I'd go through all of it all over again—and more—for you."

Megan kissed him back. "I'd rather you didn't go through anything except loving me."

22

The Big Day

NEW YEAR'S EVE, the day when everyone looked back on their past and made resolutions for a bright future. What better day for their wedding? On a cold, clear evening the Cordial Creek community gathered in Sam and Meg's church, filling it to the brim to share in a moment that had been a long time in coming. Where else could they marry except in the place of beginnings and endings, where Sam's father slept nearby, where they could feel his closeness? It was a simple ceremony with Michael for best man and Megan's friend, Sophia, as maid of honor. Poinsettias and white candles brightened the chapel while a string of candles lined the walkway outside. Their closest friends—most of the town—and family waited for them.

Sam walked down the aisle of the church with a slight limp that would eventually be cured with physical therapy. He shifted his weight to his right to ease the ache as he waited for Meg's entrance. He'd been waiting for her most of his life and still couldn't believe their wedding day was finally here. They'd come so close to losing each other. That thought still made his mouth go dry and his heart to race at the thought of it. He half expected someone to wake him up and tell him this ceremony was a dream.

Megan walked in on her father's arm, the wedding

march playing softly. The moment she saw Sam's smile and eyes so full of emotion, she felt as if there was a presence on her right side. "Thanks for coming, Dad O'Malley," she whispered. "I promise I'll take good care of him and treat him right from now on." Never again would she doubt the man standing in front of her. He was her Robin Hood, her Prince Charming, her knight in shining armor. He had taken all of those roles when they were children and continued to do so as they grew up, shining in his faith and love for her.

Sam found himself standing up straighter and taller, the throb in his leg forgotten as his heart began to pound in his ears. His Meggie, she was the stuff of fairy tales. More beautiful than he'd ever seen her before, more beautiful than any other woman in the world. He was afraid if he blinked she would disappear. Those fears were laid to rest when her father placed her hand in his. It was reassuringly warm, solid, and he wasn't letting go.

There was a shifting in the air, and the candles on the altar flickered although there was no draft. Sam knew someone was at his side even if he could not be seen. The butterflies in Sam's stomach settled, and the pounding of his heart quieted. He closed his eyes, let out the breath that he'd been holding. *I knew you'd be here, Dad. You always wanted this for me, too. I love you.* He spoke in the softest of whispers, his heart brimming with a rush of feeling that threatened to carry him away. It was as close as he would get to having his father with him; the longing to hold on to his father, look in that face so like his, almost floored Sam, but now was not the time for sadness. Happiness lived here and was here to stay.

Megan leaned in close to murmur in his ear. "I felt him, too." Sam squeezed her hand even more tightly, allowing her to be his anchor and keep him in the moment. Blessings upon blessings.

Pastor Tony waited, allowing the bride and groom to savor the moment before continuing with the service. He kept it short, simple, and sweet. There was no reason to expand on something everyone in this community had expected for a lifetime between the couple before them.

The exchange of rings took place; Meg's delicate heart-shaped diamond on her left hand and a blue ring on her right, catching all eyes. Vows followed as both she and Sam broke from tradition to voice their own.

Sam held Meg's hands in his and gazed into her eyes, his voice clear and steady. "I, Samuel O'Malley, take you Megan Taylor, to be my wife. You are my past, my present, and my future. You are all of the little things in my life, old and new. You are my familiar yesterdays and my unknown tomorrows, and I will always be true to you and our love."

Megan felt her eyes begin to tear. There was such happiness bursting inside of her, shining in her eyes and reflected in Sam's. "I, Megan Taylor, take you, Samuel O'Malley, to be my husband. All of my life, you have been my rock-steady, my safe harbor, my soft place to land. When I lost my way, you helped me find myself. You are my favorite pair of jeans, my slippers worn bare with use, my own cozy bed after a stay away, my no-place-like-home. You've been the first chapter of my life, you'll be all the in-betweens, and my last. I will always be true to you and our love."

Pastor Tony laid a gentle hand on their heads in blessing. "I now pronounce you husband and wife. You may kiss the bride, and may God always be with you."

Sam took Megan in his arms and kissed her in a way that surpassed the power of the kiss he'd used to win her on that stormy night forever ago. He bent her back, dipping her to the floor as a roar of applause and cheers filled the tiny church. Both of them felt a well of joy rush up, filling all of the empty spaces. Their cup runneth over.

The rest of that evening was spent celebrating at their reception, which was the New Year's Eve celebration for everyone in town. When they counted down and shouted, "Happy New Year," Sam and Megan only had eyes for each other. They stepped outside to stare up at the moon and the stars, their breath misting as snow began to fall. Sam wrapped Meg in his arms to keep her warm and rested his chin on her hair. "How's that for something new, Mrs. O'Malley? Even the world has a fresh start tonight."

Megan turned and kissed him, stealing his breath. "It will do, Mr. O'Malley, because I'm with you. Hold on tight and don't ever let me go."

Epilogue

IN A FAIRY-TALE house of wood and stone by a pond, wrapped in a forest, high on a hill overlooking Cordial Creek, two children scampered indoors. They were being chased by their father. One was a four-year-old girl with dark, wavy hair and coffee eyes, the other, a two-year-old boy with sun in his ringlets and the sky in his eyes. Laughter rang out, giggles, and squeals. There was a sense of welcome chaos and barely contained energy.

They ran into the living room where Megan sat on the couch. Over the mantle was a sketch of the house they lived in. Molly looked at it now. "Daddy, can you draw me a dream house like you did for Mommy?"

Sam scooped her up. "It will be your dream house, so tell me what to draw, and I'll make it your own. When you grow up, I can build it for you, and you'll be the princess."

Jake went to his mother. "Up me! Up me!" She lifted him up only to have him stretch toward the mantle. Megan stood and let him touch the treasures—a seashell, a heart-shaped rock, a journal that was a rough draft of the newest book she'd sold, a glass robin, a copy of *The Wizard of Oz*, and a picture of Sam and Megan holding hands as children.

Molly clung to her daddy's neck and yawned sleepily. "I's tired, Daddy."

He stroked her hair. "Then let's snuggle on the

couch, and Mommy will read to us." They sat down, and Molly picked up a soft teddy bear, holding it close. Sam pictured the little girl who gave it to him in the hospital, flashed back to Megan as a little girl, too. The magic of teddy bears.

They all got comfortable, tangled in a quilt and each other. Megan nestled Jake in her arm and turned to look at her husband and daughter. "What should I read?"

"One of your books, Mommy! We love yours." Molly chirped.

Megan nodded and picked up her first children's book she'd written after she quit the law firm. She turned to the first page where a little girl sat next to a little boy, eating blueberry pie on the front step.

"What matters most in the whole wide world?" the little girl asked.

"It's you," the boy answered.

"How do you know?" she asked.

Meg and Sam paused for a moment. She and Sam traded a smile. Then she read, "Because I know all of the little things about you, inside and out, and they mean everything to me."

———

Dear Looking for Love,

Did you take Sam's advice? He's right. I know from experience. If you're with someone and considering finding someone flashy and new or see that guy standing on the greener grass on the other side, think twice. Chances are that the sparkle and the thrill will wear off, and you'll be left with a stranger. Worse yet, that grass—it will wind up brown and dead!

When you fall in love with someone, take the time to get to know him until he's your friend, your best friend. He'll be the one that has seen you with your messy hair, no make-up, and morning breath at the beginning of the day. He's lived to tell the tale when you are grumpy or in a temper. YOU don't have to hide behind a mask, because he knows all of your secrets. He's the one you run to when you're in trouble, the first one you call when you are down. He'll be the one you want to go to sleep with and wake up to for the rest of your life.

Think about it. Close your eyes. Whose face do you see? Hold onto him because they don't make them like they used to, and you won't want to let him get away, not when he knows all of the little things about you that matter most of all.

Lesson learned,

Meg

About the Author

Heidi Sprouse writes romances about ordinary men who become extraordinary through their actions and the women who love them. She lives in historic Johnstown, a small upstate New York town on the fringe of the Adirondacks, with her husband, Jim, and son, Patrick. Please visit her at:

www.heidisprouse.wix.com/heidi-sprouse.

You can also go to her Facebook page, Heidi Sprouse Writing "All the Little Things" and More.

CPSIA information can be obtained at www.ICGtesting.com
Printed in the USA
BVOW08s0829120616

451696BV00002B/37/P